# ANDROID AVENGER

## Ted White

Breathing Life into Great Books

ReAnimus Press
1100 Johnson Road #16-143
Golden, CO 80402
www.ReAnimus.com

© 2019 by Ted White. All rights reserved.

ISBN-13: 9781793996909

First ReAnimus Press print edition: January, 2019

10 9 8 7 6 5 4 3 2 1

*To my mother and father.*

# I

I was shaking when I came out of the Arena.

I always feel a little shaken, but this time the tensions had wrapped my stomach in knots of pain and salty perspiration stung my neck where I had shaved only a little over an hour earlier. And, despite the heavy knot in my stomach, I felt strangely empty.

I've never been able to sort out my reactions to an Execution. The atmosphere of careful boredom, the strictly-business-as-usual air, failed to dull my senses as it did for the others. I could always taste the ozone in the air, mixed with the taste of fear — whether mine, or that of the Condemned, I never knew. My nostrils always gave an involuntary twitch at the confined odors and I felt an almost claustrophobic fear at being packed into the Arena with the other nine hundred and ninety-nine Citizens on Execution Duty.

I had been expecting my notice for several months before it finally came. I hadn't served Execution Duty for nearly two years, and since it usually figured out to once every fourteen months or so on rotation, I'd been ready for it. A little apprehensive — I always am — but ready.

At 9:00 in the morning, still only half awake (I'd purposely slept until the last minute), vaguely trying to remember the dream I'd had, I waited in front of the Arena for the ordeal to begin. Our times of arrival had been staggered in our notices, so that a long queue wouldn't tie up traffic, but as usual the checkers were slow and we were backed up a bit.

I didn't feel like waiting. Somehow I've always felt more exposed on the streets, although the brain-scanners must be more plentiful in an Arena than almost anywhere else. It's only logical that they should be. The scanners—electroencephalic pick-ups, actually—are set up to detect unusual patterns of stress in our brain waves as we pass close to them, and thus to pick out as quickly as possible those with incipient or developing neuroses or psychoses—the potential Deviates. And where else would such aberrations be as likely to come out as in the Arena?

Often I had wondered why my own fears had not triggered one of the devices, and signaled the Proctors to come and take me. I *knew* my own feelings of insecurity—they bordered on paranoia at times. Yet, I'd escaped unscathed for the first thirty years of my life. Why?

Morbid thoughts like these kept flashing through my mind as I waited, and then I had moved to the front of the short line. I flashed my notification of duty to the checker, and was waved on in. I sank into the plush depth of my seat with a sigh. It was on the aisle in the "T" section, as usual.

Once this had been a first-run Broadway theater—first a place where great plays were shown, and then later the more degenerate motion pictures. Those had been times of vicarious escape from reality—times when the populace had ruled, and yet the masses had averted their eyes from the world. Many changes had come since then, with the coming of regulated sanity and the achievement of world peace. Gone now were the black arts of forgetfulness, those media which practiced the enticement of the Citizen into irresponsible escape—or so they said. Now this crowded theater was only a reminder.

And a place of execution for those who would once have sought escape here.

Perhaps thirty people were sitting on the floor of the Arena, where once there had been a stage. They sat quietly in chairs not so different from mine, strapped for the moment into a kind of passive conformity. My eyes were drawn to them—their strangeness had always exerted a perverse sort of attraction over me. As usual, most of them were young—from about ten into the early twenties. Their kind never lasted far past puberty. These were the rebels, the potential enemies of society. Criminals. Probably some of them hadn't yet realized it. But they were on the verge of antisocial insanity, and the brain-scanners had singled them out. Now society would deal with them.

A flurry of movement at the gates caught my eye. Apparently at least one of them was a full-fledged Rebel. He was struggling furiously, and three proctors were having an awkward time getting him into the Arena without hurting him.

Then, as they moved into the floodlights, I saw with a faint shock that it was a girl.

She was dressed in man's clothing, but betrayed by her unsanitary and neurotically long hair.

Long, blonde hair. For a moment I forgot where I was, and allowed myself to revel in this nearly forbidden sight. The soft waves fell halfway down her back, disarrayed now, wildly framing a face whose fierce criminality seemed to illumine her features with a fire and beauty almost beyond my recollection.

My eyes were caught by the shining highlights of her hair as the floodlights stirred it in a gentle mockery of sunlight. Something within me responded, and...

I felt a bright hot tension in my eyes, and then suddenly the scene on the floor below sharpened, and I felt as though I was hovering in mid-air directly over the defiant girl.

They were strapping her into one of the chairs, carefully pulling the soft leather straps with their attached metal electrodes around her, pinioning her. One set joined her arms to the armrests, another her legs to the specially devised footrests. Her tunic was opened—one of the proctors mumbled an apology—and a third set was passed around her chest, the metal plate fastened just under her left breast.

And then she was alone.

I stared at her, drawn magnetically to her eyes.

Strange eyes; light blue irises, surrounded by a ring of dark blue, and flecked with gold. They were shining. She had been crying, the stains still on her cheeks. No longer aware of the chair I was sitting in, or the physical distance which separated us, I looked deeper into her eyes, and they seemed to melt, like a pool of clear water growing deeper. I could almost see into, beyond them—into the darkness beyond.

Her eyes widened as she became aware of me, and then she returned my look, her unvoiced appeal probing deep within me.

Suddenly I could no longer see her. I felt a wrenching twist, and found myself once more sitting in my seat high above. A citizen settled himself down into the seat immediately before mine, restoring my sight of the floor below.

Sweat poured down my face, my clothes seemed plastered to my body. I glanced to my right, but the Citizen beside me had noticed nothing. Surreptitiously, I touched my sleeve to my face, and felt my cheeks flush.

Then, before I could look below again, the lights dimmed and rebrightened. I could feel the casual air depart from the place. All around me Citizens straightened in their seats. My hand moved out involuntarily to the board in front of me, and I stared down at it.

A very simple set-up, of course—nothing more complicated is needed—a bulb and a pushbutton. You wait until the bulb lights, and then your thumb or forefinger, which has been straining over the button, plunges down, jabbing almost viciously. That is, it does if you're me, Bob Tanner. My neighbors' hands moved with bored precision. One thousand little blue bulbs lit with half a watt or less of electricity. And one thousand relays—assuming all the buttons were alive, something one could not take for granted—clicked over, each endeavoring to be the first to unloose the tide of electricity which would sweep over the stoic dolls on the floor below.

I watched my hand move, unbidden, over the vicious little button, and with a feeling of horror I saw the little blue light snap on.

*Let it be me, and not one of those automatons!* I thought to myself, stabbing painfully at the pushbutton.

The overhead lights, momentarily drained, dimmed again, the seated figures below jerked for a few seconds, and then it was all over. Our pushbuttons were as dead as they'd been at our entrance and our power as executioners was gone. At least for the next twelve months.

I climbed jerkily to my feet, the catharsis of the experience I'd just undergone leaving me drained of my own energy, and waited for the row behind me to empty. When its last man moved out into the aisle, I followed him up the aisle and down the steps to the exit.

Something always hit me when I left the Arena, leaving the faded red plush and soft lights for the brightly sunlit world of 2017. Usually it would be a fairly common sort of after-reaction, a nervous exhaustion, first in the knees and then in the pit of my stomach, and I would start to shake. I didn't have to be told this was a neurotic attitude, and the very fear of this only reinforced the reaction.

This time—this time I could not snap out of it. The world seemed unreal, out of focus, blurred around the edges and paper-thin. The intensity of my experience made even the bright sunlight pale. It had never happened like this before — *what was happening to me?*

Still not under control, I stepped from the sidewalk onto the moving street and damn near killed myself.

## II

The moving roads are still found only in the largest cities. New York, London, Tokyo, are the only ones to my knowledge. New York's are the oldest, thirty years old now. I doubt we'd ever have had moving roads if it hadn't been for the ban on vehicular traffic in 1982, when they finished the new freight and passenger subway system. Originally the idea had been for some short-haul transit to fill in the gaps between subway stations, and the streets would be planted with grass while the moving strips went underground along with nearly everything else. But in those days we still had politics to contend with, and the disclosure of the huge swindle perpetrated by the Independent Party machine—grafting almost the entirety of a fifteen-million-dollar bond issue—pretty well ruled out any more underground construction. By then, what with sewers, water mains, central heating mains gas and electricity mains, and the new transit network, Manhattan was honeycombed underground. To construct a new underground network of moving passenger belts would've eaten up that fifteen million for a starter, and taken many times more for completion. The Mayor of New York—an Independent man—was no fool. He used the one avenue open for escape: he built the moving streets on the surface, where the former streets had been.

The result is that in Manhattan we have the only beltways exposed to the elements, and, naturally, the only beltways which close down at the first sign of inclement weather. Even a mild shower will stop them, ever since a woman slipped on a wet street and sued the city to a fare-thee-well. Nowadays, of course, no one would think of pressing suit against anyone else; there is no corruption in the city government, and indeed there is very little government of any kind. The citizenry is sane, after all.

Or so they teach in school.

The moving roads are set up as a series of endless belts side by side, the one closest to the sidewalk moving at five miles an hour, and each one over moving five miles an hour faster. On a wide avenue, like Sixth, you can get a center strip which goes up to 20 miles an hour. Not excitingly fast, but fast enough, since it never stops.

You learn to move from strip to strip easily; just brace your legs and shove forward with the one on the slower strip as you step over. If you've known the beltways ever since you were a child, as I have, it's completely a matter of reflex and instinct. I could do it blindfolded.

But not after that execution.

Somehow I managed to step half onto the street and half onto the sidewalk. The sudden twist threw me into the air, and as I fell, I could feel some huge, mindless monster chewing on my leg.

The next thing I knew, I was in a hospital.

I was numb, that was all I could tell about myself. A red haze covered my surroundings. I was lying on my back, against something hard.

"This one's a case, all right!" said a voice almost directly behind my left ear.

My heart leapt with sudden panic. I tried to rise, to sit up. Nothing happened. I was completely helpless; I could not move.

I should not have been conscious. My body was in a state of drugged torpor, and I realized suddenly that my eyes were closed. The redness was the light which penetrated my eyelids.

It made no sense for me to be conscious, but I was, reasoning and receptive. I could hear and feel.

"Look at that leg," said another voice. "Ripped right up the thigh."

"Any fractures?"

"I'm setting up the machine. We'll know in a minute."

There was a hum from overhead, and my scalp prickled, although I knew it could only be an X-ray machine.

Then a door opened and closed, and I waited. There was no time for me, only an endless suspension of experience. For a while I could hear one of the men clicking and clinking what I imagined to be surgical instruments in some other part of the room, and then there was only silence. I had no way of knowing how long it had been when I heard the door slam open and an excited voice say, "Henry! Take a good look at this!"

I wished desperately I could open my eyes.

"You must have made a wrong setting."

"Wrong setting, hell! Look at the rest of the print. I—"

"Easy, easy. Let's stay calm. You know..."

I knew too. The brain-scanners would not be absent here.

"Hmmm, that *is* strange, yes."

"Yeah, Henry. Look at the bones. Sure, they're whole, no fractures, not even chipping. *But bones don't photograph like that.* They don't cast that sort of shadow on an X-ray. No marrow, no depth—just a completely solid image. Like a hunk of metal."

"You're right. Absolutely right. But we need confirmation. More shots. Do his entire body."

I felt the cart I was on being shifted. The motion set my mind reeling. My bones didn't look like bones? What were they talking about? There was nothing unusual about my legs that I could recall. I'd had no operations, no broken bones, nothing artificial added. *What was happening to me?*

I could feel something large and warm being lowered closer to my body, and then they began the process of photographing me from head to toe, plate by plate.

They were absent for a long while after that.

I had been drifting, dreaming those peculiar waking-dreams of free-association and shifting images one usually has before falling completely asleep. There was something about a man, the same man I'd dreamed about earlier. He was gross-bodied and bald-headed. He was doing something. I couldn't tell what. His face was distorted into a malicious grin. Then I heard the voices close by again, and was fully awake.

"There's one immediate test, that's all," said a voice. "If we find what we expect to find, we'll have to make a report."

I felt something tugging at my left leg, and then felt a soundless vibration transmitted up my leg as something smooth and sharp slid along my bone.

"Look at that," said the voice. "Metal."

I blacked out.

When I came to again I felt quite different. I could feel again.

I was lying in a hospital bed, a sheet pulled over me to my chin. My left leg felt encased in something. And it itched. I started to reach one hand down to touch it when I heard the door latch click.

I had barely time to return to my original position before I heard several men enter the room.

I opened my eyes to thin slits and looked around.

The room was a small private cubicle painted a dull, neutral color. Immediately at my side stood two men, one dressed in white, the other in a light business suit.

Business Suit spoke. "Doesn't look abnormal... Let's have a closer look at him."

"Yes sir. I just put his leg in a temporary plastic job," said the other in a voice I recognized as being Henry's. He pulled the sheet from over my leg. I couldn't see what he was doing, but suddenly the pressure on my leg ceased, and more than anything I desperately wanted to scratch myself. But I held myself in check.

There was a muffled exclamation.

"Sir! I swear to you, we had the entire femur exposed down to the kneecap!"

There was a long silence. I could imagine Henry sweating to himself.

"A sane mind is an open mind," said Business Suit, mostly to himself. "Is he still under sedation?" he asked after a pause.

"Yes sir. We've been keeping him on ice until a decision was made."

"I want to see those plates again," the other said, and shortly the door had closed behind them again.

For a short time I lay stunned by what I'd heard. Then, tentatively, I reached down to feel my leg.

They'd left the casing off. I slid my hand down my thigh slowly, expecting at any moment to reach the wound. My hand encountered only smooth flesh all the way down to my knee.

I sat bolt upright.

Throwing the sheet off me, I stared down at my body.

My left leg was whole, as whole and healthy as my right leg.

But—I had *felt* the scalpel peel away the flesh from my leg, felt it scrape along the bone. And the whole leg had been torn up—hadn't it?—from my accident.

I stared at the leg.

If you looked for it, you could see the fresh skin. There was no scar, but the new skin was a lighter pink, and as yet hairless. It extended in rough patches down the outer side of my leg. I fingered it. It felt normal, perhaps smoother, but the skin had feeling of its own; it was not dead.

I ran my hands over my leg, fascinated, for many long minutes. Then consciousness of what this meant began to reach me.

*I was different.* How different I had no way of knowing. But I had a metal leg bone, very possibly metal bones throughout. (But blood cells are manufactured in the bones' marrow. How *could* I have all metal bones? It was one more question for the list.) And I appeared to be able to regenerate flesh over a fresh wound in a matter of hours. And what had they said about my being "on ice"? I had thrown off the effects of whatever drug they'd administered me.

*What was I?*

Well, that was one question I wanted to be able to answer at my leisure, and I knew that I wouldn't care for *their* answer. Perhaps cases of "physical deviancy" were far rarer than those of mental deviancy, but I'd heard stories of the occasional mutant still being born: residual payments for the heavy blanket of radiation unleashed by the war mongers of the Twentieth Century and the populace's mad dabblings with untested drugs. But those poor unfortunates rarely lasted past their early infancy before execution.

The hospital was no place for me. At any moment they might reach their decision and send the proctors for me. The only point in my favor for the moment was the fact that they thought I was under wraps for the time being. It was time to do something while I still had that advantage.

Cautiously I tested my strength against the bed, and raised myself to a sitting position. I felt weak, but not too weak to navigate.

Problem Number One: clothes. I was naked.

I rose and on still uncertain feet, prowled the room.

It was just a cubicle. Barely big enough for the bed, a night stand, and a chair, and space for three or four visitors. There was no closet, no clothes thrown over the chair. I had hardly expected to find any. They hadn't figured I was in immediate need of any.

I tried the door. Unlocked. No reason, of course, why it shouldn't be. If I were a normal human being I wouldn't have even been able to raise my eyelids.

I pulled the door open, and stared down a long, sterile, empty hallway, lined with closed doors identical with mine. This was no good. No good at all.

Somewhere in this vast building would be my clothes, but where, I had no idea. In fact, I had no idea where I was. Nor even the name of the hospital. It didn't leave me much.

I hovered uncertainly in the doorway, my naked body covered with goosebumps. Then, suddenly, the door directly opposite me opened.

I jumped back, but too slowly. A young man, dressed in street clothes, stared at me for a pair of seconds, then leaped forward.

I knew what to do, then.

As I stepped awkwardly back into my room, I let myself go limp, collapsing upon the floor.

The man stooped down over me. "What's happening here?" he asked no one in particular. "We've got to get you back in bed!"

I let him bend over me until his face was inches from mine, and he was preparing to slip his hands under my shoulders and lift me.

Then I chopped him. I gave him a fast rabbit punch on the back of his neck. He collapsed on top of me, momentarily pinning me with his limp body.

Trembling, I pulled myself out from under him, and rose for the door. Once it was closed and locked, I returned to him, and began methodically stripping him.

If I were to pinpoint the moment in space and time that I became overtly antisocial, it would be then. That was when I made my first conscious decision to act against another. For a moment

I felt a constriction of conscience and debated my course of action.

But I had no course. Society had already condemned me. Once my difference had been discovered society and I could no longer co-exist. I was now a point of contagion. I must be destroyed—if they could.

There's no reason, I suppose, why in a world of mental conformity there should also be physical conformity, but yet there is. The "average" is elastic enough to permit a few who are a good bit taller or shorter, but only a very few. Perhaps their physical abnormality pushes these "deviates" into emotional rebellion and true mental deviancy; I wouldn't know. But right now I was grateful that over 90 % of the world's male population was within three inches of the same height, and that in my age bracket I could probably swap clothes with most of them.

This fellow was a little stockier than I, but he was almost exactly my height. I had no trouble whatsoever with his clothes, although it took me a moment to decide to wear his underwear.

The clothes on, I ran my fingers through my hair for a moment in lieu of a comb, and then stepped out into the hall.

Almost immediately, I backed into the room again. I was being stupid; found on the floor, the nude body of my unwitting benefactor would be instant cause for alarm. On the other hand, my chances might be greatly improved if he was in the bed.

It was the work of only a few short moments to tuck him into the bed I had so recently vacated. I turned his head away from the door, arranged the open plastic casing around his left leg, and pulled the covers up close around his neck. To anyone only peeking into the room there would seem to be nothing wrong.

Feeling rather smug about that extra touch, I slipped back out into the hall and closed the door. It occurred to me when I was halfway down the hall that in this blankly antiseptic corridor it would be almost impossible for me to find this room again myself.

Just around the corner of the intersection of my hall and another, I found a bank of elevators. There was a small passenger elevator, the button for which I pushed nervously, and beside it the wide doors of a service-type elevator. The patients would be wheeled into that one and taken down to the operating levels.

I had been fidgeting for several moments when the doors slid soundlessly open and I stepped into the elevator.

I turned to face the doors, and glanced up at the strip of numbers over them. Eighty-two was lighted. There was only one hospital that tall—I was in the Greater Bellevue. It was not encouraging information.

The doors had closed, but the elevator hung motionless. Where did I want to go? Directly to the first floor? I would be running a risk, I decided, if I emerged without warning directly on the main floor. It would be easy for them to have someone stationed at the elevator, waiting. Better to take a higher floor and walk down the last flight. I punched Two, and the floor momentarily dropped from under me.

We stopped to pick up three male nurses on the fifty-seventh floor, but there were no other passengers. The nurses glanced at me idly, but without curiosity. Apparently I hadn't blundered into a private staff elevator—but then, that hardly seemed likely.

The nurses got off at the fifth floor, which I gathered from their casual conversation held the operating arenas, and when the elevator stopped again with the Two lit above the doors, there was no one with me to witness my cautious departure.

I was in an alcove which opened upon a vast lounge, warmly furnished with thick, pile carpets, comfortable-looking chairs, smoking stands, lamps, and low tables scattered about. There weren't many people in the room, and none of them seemed to be paying any attention to me.

I began looking about for an exit.

"Pardon me, sir. Are you a member of the Staff?"

The voice was almost directly in my ear, and I jumped.

"I beg your pardon," she repeated. "I didn't mean to startle you."

"I'm sorry," I said, turning, "I'm not familiar with—"

"I'm afraid you must've gotten off at the wrong floor," she said, and I took a better look at the young woman who had intercepted me. She did not look over twenty, and her appearance was striking, especially in this day of mass-produced features. Her hair was a deep glowing red, and she was so short she stood barely even with my chin. She wore glasses which added a pertness to her face and did not hide her lovely green-hued eyes. Her eyes were wide apart, but her high cheekbones and full, generous lips created a slightly exotic Indo-European look. She wore her hair pageboy, with bangs low on her forehead. She looked totally out of place in this setting.

"The wrong floor..." I repeated after her with vague pomposity. "Dear me, I'm most sorry. I'm a visitor.... I was just leaving," I added.

She glanced sharply at me for a moment, but seemed reassured by my anonymous features and apparent health. I was nobody, one of thousands of nobodies she must encounter daily.

"I'll show you to the stairs," she said, and then led me around another corner to another alcove which opened upon a wide carpeted stair leading down to a closed set of doors.

"They open on the main lobby," she said, gesturing downwards.

"Thank you," I said, mechanically.

"Not at—"

A soft but penetrating voice interrupted her. "Attention, please. Attention, please. A patient is missing from Room AA, floor Eighty-two. The patient was involved in a severe accident involving contusions and lacerations of the hips and thighs, and was under heavy sedation. He should not have been moved under any circumstances. There is suspicion of physical deviancy. Any persons having knowledge of the case please report immediately. Thank you."

"My goodness," I said, slightly fatuously. "They certainly have the speakers well hidden." I peered nearsightedly at the ceiling and corners, pretending to see nothing. Then I let my concentration narrow upon the area from which my ears told me the sound had come, and found it. My vision sharpened as I seemed to zoom up on what I'd found—an old trick I'd discovered years earlier and unconsciously used in the Arena. The walls had been covered with what first appeared to be a textured wallpaper, but was actually a fabric which served the function of speaker grill cloth over the speaker itself. I could just make out the square outline of an inset electrostatic speaker. Damned clever, I had to admit. And if there were speakers hidden in the walls, who knew what else they might have...?

The girl was observing me closely, so I shrugged as though baffled, and allowed myself to be guided down the stairs.

At the bottom, she turned to me and in a quiet undertone she said, "If I were you, I'd be very careful."

# III

I stared at the girl as she turned and mounted the stairs. She presented a pleasant view, but my mind was not on it. I shook my head, turned, and gently pushed one of the doors.

The lobby was full of bustling people, most of them dressed as I was. There seemed to be a larger than normal proportion of white-jacketed men near the main desk, and several proctors standing idly around the elevator banks, but none of them were looking in my direction and no one else seemed interested in me, so I sauntered free of the door and quickly mingled with the stream of people moving towards the large revolving doors.

Suddenly I was aware of two proctors, flanking the doorway. Each held in his hand a small device not unlike an old-fashioned light meter in appearance. Each pointed it at each person who passed by him.

My blood froze, and for a moment I faltered. I knew what those "meters" were: portable scanners linked into the main scanning complex, which in turn fed the central administration computer-complex. Those slim little gadgets were fully capable of picking up a deviating brain wave, feeding it into the main circuits, receiving a positive response, and identifying the deviate in a few microseconds. Normally proctors used them to assure themselves that they did indeed have the criminal they'd been sent for. But, used up close like this, they were fully as efficient as the larger, fixed scanners, for spot checks.

*What was I going to do?* There were only two men in front of me now, and in a moment I'd be directly confronted by one of those damned scanners.

With the big ones, hidden who-knows-where, there's always the chance of being skipped over, and up to now I'd always known this was what'd happened to me. Now would come the direct confrontation — *now!*

The proctor on my right pointed the little black instrument at me, a bored expression on his face. I halted, waiting for his reaction, for the double-take of surprise which would sweep over him, and readying myself to hit him, to make some sort of break.

There was a nudge from behind me, and the proctor said, impatiently, "Pass on, Citizen," and waved me on with his hand. Then I was through the doors and on the moving street.

I headed uptown on First Avenue. I had no specific destination in mind. My only thought was to remain within a group, to remain inconspicuous. I paid no attention to my surroundings. I couldn't get my mind off what had just happened.

*The scanners had passed me.*

Every citizen thinks of himself as two people. On the one hand, he knows, in his own heart, that he's an Innocent. He's good, he's sane, he's a productive citizen. And yet — and yet, who can help feeling at least a little furtive guilt? Who can refrain from cringing when passing a known scanner? *Will it happen this time?* he asks himself. Who can truly say with certainty that he's sane? We have only the negative evidence: the scanners have not singled us out. *But maybe up till now they've overlooked me.* Will they pick me *next* time?

But most citizens take great care to avoid the sort of thoughts which might command a scanner's attention. And to actually commit an act of aggression...

Up to now I too had thought as the average citizen had — I felt the duality of innocence and guilt, and remained half convinced that I was free only because no scanner had ever been properly focused upon me. But in that hospital I had done something no one could do and safely pass the scanners — and the scanners had registered nothing. It was unbelievable. What did it mean?

It was amazing how fast they'd discovered my absence, too. I'd thought I would get at least an hour or two's leeway out of my little subterfuge. How had they caught on so fast?

Lastly, there was the girl. *Who was she,* and what did she mean by her cryptic warning? Did she know who I was? But that would be impossible. I'd never seen her before.

I was at about Twenty-ninth Street, and I nearly lost my balance again, when I figured out one answer: the obvious one. They'd missed me because they had a scanner in my room.

Never mind the fact that the scanner didn't register when I left the building. Obviously they'd put me in a room with one; it would be the first thing they'd do as soon as they realized my physical deviancy. It was unlikely they'd had anyone directly monitoring it — they must've felt safe about my physical immobility at least — but they probably kept tabs on me every hour or so to see if I'd returned to consciousness yet, and, if I had, if I'd betrayed any mental deviations.

There was no way of knowing what had tipped them to the imposter in my bed, but obviously the scanner had picked something up. And what consternation it must've caused them to find me gone! They wouldn't know for sure whether I'd succeeded in handling my escape alone or whether I'd had help. Their reports of my physical condition would be contradictory and of little help, but judging from the announcement I'd heard over the PA, they still considered me a wheelchair case at best, and had figured on outside help.

I should've thought of a scanner in my room before. I was lucky such stupidity hadn't already tripped me up. It was time I began thinking ahead a little, instead of reacting blindly.

Moving more carefully than usual, and acutely sensitive to the motions of the people around me, I changed belts and stepped onto solid pavement at Thirty-first Street.

The small shops were busy with the late afternoon crowd off from work. It was already 3:30, I discovered. I wished I still had my own watch; it had been taken from me and the man I'd robbed hadn't worn one.

I stepped into one of the corner telephone booths and punched my own number.

After three rings a voice answered gruffly, "Tanner."

"Is Mr. Tanner there?" I inquired innocently.

"Speaking," said the voice.

"Bob?" I asked. "Got a cold? That doesn't sound like you, boy." I laughed.

*"Who is this, please?"*

"And just who is *this?*" I countered.

"Just one moment, please," said the voice. "I'll see if he's here."

"Who—?" I asked, and then I got it. Without hanging up, I dropped the phone the length of its cord, and moved quickly out of the booth. I grabbed the first man to pass me, impatiently, and gestured him into the booth. He entered it uncomprehendingly and reached for the dangling phone as I pointed at it and said, "It's for you, Citizen."

I was almost a block away and about to turn the corner when, casually glancing back, I saw three proctors converge on the booth.

I was certainly becoming a dangerous deviant, I reflected, causing innocent people so much trouble.

I'd found out something important. There was no use heading for home. They'd identified me and were in my apartment. The proctor who'd answered the phone had been stalling me, not because he needed to trace the call—that had been instantaneous—but in order to hold me for pickup.

It was damned curious, when I thought about it again, that they'd had so little luck finding me. What was wrong with the brain scanners, anyway? Or were my thoughts the thoughts of the pure despite all?

Somehow I doubted that like hell.

Where to go? I dug into my pockets, and one hand emerged with a wallet. As casually as I could among the pedestrian traffic, I inspected it.

The ID was for Charles L. Simpson. There was an address too, but I decided not to bother with it. It was a cinch they'd have that sewed up too.

Where to go? It was still a big country. The first step was to get out of the population concentration of Manhattan. If I headed for Staten Island, I could move from there to New Jersey, and then I could strike west into Pennsylvania and lose myself easily in the rural mountain districts. It was impossible to maintain scanners and close thought-control in such loosely populated districts, I knew, and besides population pressures were commonly thought to cause most mental deviation and crime. The farming areas, with their much greater contact with the healthy outdoors world, were much saner. That way lay freedom.

The first step was down.

I had been walking uptown. At Thirty-fourth Street, I stepped onto the escalator leading down into the subway system.

Let no one tell you there's a finer subway in any city than that in New York. It's quite true that other cities have better beltways, and the new landscaping in London makes it a far more beautiful city than New York will ever be—and I know that many will say it always was—but, after 1982, when the new subway system was finished, New York's boast in that department has gone unchallenged.

The basic concept of any large and living city must include rapid transit. One must be able to move quickly and easily from one part of the city to any other part. Otherwise the city suffers a hardening of its arteries and dies of congestion.

Private vehicles were the accepted mode in the pre-sanity days, and they were a striking example of the insanity of millions of people all trying to act as individuals. They caused so many jams, they clogged the thoroughfares so completely that not only could the citizens not get about easily, but vital freight and goods could not be transported and delivered easily either.

The master subway plan was designed to cope with this.

It was decided to provide a subway system so comprehensive that—except for the beltways—no other means of transportation would be needed in Manhattan. This meant putting lines under almost every avenue which didn't already have one, and connecting these with frequent crosstown shuttle lines. It meant honeycombing the island with those roaring underground trains.

The plan also called for three levels to the new subways. On the top level run the local and express trains, the locals stopping nearly every five blocks, the expresses every fifteen blocks. Below these are the high-speed limited-express tracks, with stations roughly fifty blocks apart, sometimes more. These trains run better than ninety miles an hour, in contrast to the forty-five mph top on the upper-level trains, and can cover ten or fifteen miles in an amazingly short commuting time. This is important, since most of Manhattan's working population lives in one of the other boroughs.

Below this level is a third level, and one the New Yorker rarely thinks of unless his work brings him into contact with it. This is the freight level. Down there run continuous freight trains, constantly loading and unloading at the platforms which stretch along the outer tracks, disgorging goods which are carried from platform to the individual shipping or receiving departments by conveyer or elevator. It is upon these lines, and these lines solely, that Manhattan's commerce depends. Trucking is a thing of the past.

Because of this master plan, Manhattan now ranks at the top of all urban areas in transit efficiency, and the results of this have been noticeable upon the populace. "Pressure eased is sanity gained," as they say.

When I stepped off the escalator I was caught in the homeward bound crowds exactly as I planned. There was no other way to get to Staten Island, of course, and I would have to use the subway in any case, but in crowds like these it would be much harder for either the ubiquitous scanners or any watching proctors to pick me out. And once on the more suburban Staten Island I would have a much easier time of it.

I was already planning my route from Staten Island when I changed from the crosstown shuttle at Sixth Avenue for the downtown Limited Express, and stepped into the streamlined, low-slung air-conditioned car.

I had barely gotten myself seated and comfortable when the train began to glide from the station. The luxurious train contrasted sharply with the perennially dingy subway station, and I relaxed as we quickly gathered speed. One more stop, downtown, at Wall Street, and then we'd be heading beneath Governor's Island and out under the bay.

The whispering of the tunnel walls shooting past joined with the sibilant sound of the air-conditioning, soothing and lulling me. I glanced up at the TV screen at the front of the car and regarded it without interest.

As usual a parade of commercials were pouring silently across the wide screen. The constant flicker of movement made it almost impossible to keep one's eye from them, and most of the other passengers gazed with a bored hypnotic stare at the screen. I knew these commercials helped keep our fare down to a quarter, but I found little else to recommend them. Every half hour, should anyone be really noticing, he'd see a brief newscast—brief mostly because a sane world is a dull world; nothing ever really happens—and a weathercast, and then without pause the commercials would resume.

We were just pulling into Wall Street when my face appeared on the screen.

I'd had just time to recognize it as an old photo from my ID card before I'd stepped out of the car.

The hairs on the back of my neck were tingling, and I moved quickly away from the train. Had anyone noticed? I didn't think so. Few would pay that much attention to the newscast in the first place, and in any case a New Yorker *never* takes any notice of his fellow riders. Still, it paid not to risk overexposing myself.

I seemed to be moving more quickly than usual. The train, as it slid away from the station, seemed to be slowing down. I tried to stop to watch it.

Without volition, my body turned and the scene whirled before my eyes. I felt a moment of vertigo, and my heart seemed to be pounding in my skull.

As I moved among them the other passengers standing on the platform seemed rooted to their places. One began to lift his foot with infinitesimal care, but I could barely glance at him from the corner of my eye before I was past him.

I was in a nightmare. Behind me I heard a train begin to creep into the station, and then I was threading my way between the immobile bodies stationed on the stairs.

*What was happening to me?* A prisoner in my own body, I watched myself vault the chain on an unused escalator, and run up it, past the unprotesting multitude on its silent nearby twin. It took me only seconds to reach the top of the six flights. My body seemed to be flying.

Then I was out of the station and moving down Fulton Street.

I was pounding down a crowded street at better than forty miles an hour. The wind ripped at my clothes, sweeping my hair and fluttering my eyes. My reaction rate was equal to my running speed. My body saw and evaluated situations instantly, enabling me to weave easily among the clumps of people who were clogging the street. My entire metabolism was enormously speeded up—I wasn't even breathing heavily.

My body seemed to be functioning automatically. It was as though I were the helpless passenger in a runaway car. Deliberately I tried—a tremendous act of conscious will—to slow myself down or throw myself off balance.

Nothing. I—the self that thought, that felt, that contained the ego and was *me*—had no control at all. Something else had assumed control and was guiding me, running, dodging, exercising complex skills I'd never known, controlling and compensating for my vastly increased inertia—

If I'd hit anyone, it would've killed us.

Three blocks down Fulton Street, plunging through the man-made canyons which once symbolized power and now meant nothing more than that buildings were still useful for the office forces which implemented the administration of the nation, I slowed down to what now seemed to me a dreary crawl. My senses still ran at a higher speed, but my body had slowed itself so that I could turn easily into the door of an anonymously nondescript office building.

The revolving door dragged through molasses and I spent an eternity leaning, barely moving, waiting to reach the inside. Then my body speeded up again, and, pausing only momentarily for the door to the fire stairs, I found myself climbing, bounding upwards at five steps a time, jumping twice to each landing.

The skin was wearing badly from my hands as I rounded the last turn, one hand swinging on the railing, the other bracing against the wall, and I shot out the door onto the Twenty-third floor.

Without a pause, my body turned left, and sped down the corridor. I had barely time to scan the name on the door, "Tabulating Dept., Subdistrict C, New York," before hearing it smash against the wall behind me, the tinkle of shards of glass falling to the floor barely reaching my ears as I moved through the room beyond.

It was late, and there was no one in the first several rooms, but when I had plunged through them to the final room in the suite, I surprised a man sitting at a console.

I noticed, with the detached part of my mind which noticed everything, that he was not very old—perhaps in his late thirties—was wearing a conventional black business suit with quarter-inch lapels, and was apparently typing a new program into his console. The console, of course, would be connected with the vast computer-complex which coordinated administrative control.

His reflexes were good. He had just started to look up before I killed him.

He'd begun to swing around in his chair when my mouth opened, and a thin, deep, blood-red ray shot out, transfixing the man. The tight thin beam carved through his smoking body, cleaving him head to abdomen as I nodded, wreaking havoc on a good portion of the console behind him as well. The odor of ozone and burned flesh hung heavily in the air, and I felt like vomiting.

My mouth closed, and I stopped dead and just stood there, blinking. It was all over. I had control over myself again.

I stumbled back through two rooms to a small washroom and was sick.

# IV

The taste of bile still bitter in my mouth, I returned to my victim, and began going through his pockets.

The questions were piling up too fast for me. Too much was going on which I couldn't explain. Now the list was topped by murder.

His wallet contained his ID card. His name was Anton Wilson. It meant nothing to me.

I shuffled through the remaining papers in his wallet. There was very little: a few cryptic notes written to himself, apparently about his work, a pocket appointment book, a few business cards, and a pocket calendar. The wallet was hanging loosely in my hand when I felt something else. The back of the wallet was stiffer in one spot. I lifted the flap, and found under it a photograph, laminated in plastic.

It was a good photo—color, and an excellent likeness, even to the shade of her deep red hair.

The girl at the hospital.

There was no doubt of it; she was impossible to mistake. The reverse of the photo had been inscribed, before lamination. It said, *With fondest memories, Hoyden.*

"Hoyden" means "rude woman." A curious name for a girl in this modern age of enlightened reality. I wondered if it was her real name.

I turned it back over and stared at her likeness. Her eyes seemed to stare directly at me, looking at me in the same knowing way she had at the hospital.

Then I heard glass tinkling and crunching as someone entered the suite of offices. I slipped the photo into my shirt pocket, looked about futilely for a place to hide, then started for the door.

We met almost at the door. She turned the corner of the corridor, and stared at me coldly and with no sign of surprise. In her hand was a stun gun.

For a moment I thought she was Hoyden—her hair was almost the same shade of red. But she was taller, slimmer. She was wearing very fashionable clothes: slacks, a vest, a severely tailored suit coat, over a ruffled white blouse. A bow-string tie caught up the blouse at her neck. The clothing fit her like a suede glove. She was very attractive—or would have been, if her face wasn't so frozen cold, and the gun hadn't been in her hand.

I backed a short retreat into the room again, the sharp metallic taste still in my throat. I wanted to clear my throat, but only swallowed.

Her eyes swept the room, cataloguing its contents as an adding machine might, and dwelling upon Wilson's body quite impersonally. Her face could have been a wax mask. Neither of us spoke.

Finally, she centered her attention upon me again.

"Why'd you kill him?" she asked. Her voice was low, its warmth in odd contrast to her expression.

"I didn't," I said. "He was dead when I got here."

"He was burned," she said. "I'll have to search you."

"Hold on a minute," I said. "Who are you? What gives you any right—?"

"This," she said, gesturing with the gun, "gives me all the right I need. Now, do you want to be searched conscious or unconscious? I understand you can wake up with quite a hangover."

"I can do without that," I said, shrugging. "Go ahead. But where'd you get the gun? Only proctors are supposed to have—"

She was uninterested in the contents of my pockets, satisfying herself by patting me quite impersonally wherever my clothing hung loose. She didn't find what she was looking for. She straightened up and stared at me, slightly puzzled. Then she crossed over to the window, and tugged at it. It was sealed, the building air-conditioned.

"I suppose you could've ditched it somewhere in this room," she said, almost under her breath.

"Ditched what?" I asked.

"The laser. The laser he was burned with," she said, nodding at Wilson.

She was making me more and more curious about herself. "Just who *are* you?" I asked.

"Barbara Wilson," she said. She nodded at the figure on the floor. "His sister."

She took me to her apartment. It was uptown, overlooking the Park, on the east. It was a large apartment, part of what had once been a town house, back in a time when there was a moneyed class which indulged in such things. It was still more than a cut above the usual apartment. There seemed to be several bedrooms off a hall which led to the rear of the house, and we'd passed through a dining room to reach the large front room. The walls were covered with an expensive fabric that was faintly iridescent in the late afternoon sunshine that slanted warm yellow rays through the windows. The neatly fitted blocks of the parquet floor caught the sunlight and held it impatterned. I walked across the room, and stared out the high windows at the trees of the park. Below Citizens strolled down along the plaza that had been Fifth Avenue. Beyond the fringe of trees, I could see the tall, shining, featureless block that housed the computer-complex.

"Well, here we are," I said at last, turning away from the window and facing the girl. "Now what?"

"Now you tell me all about the death of Anton Wilson," she replied.

"You remind me of someone," I said. "She had red hair too."

"Many do," she said impatiently.

"Anton knew her, too."

The ringing phone cut off her reply to that one.

"Hello? Yes... yes, I know. I was there. No, not when it happened, but shortly afterwards. It was done with a laser. Yes. Yes, I think I may. I'll let you know." She hung up the phone and turned on me. "Enough is enough. Who are you, and what were you doing there?"

"The name is Simpson, Charles Simpson," I said. "I was just there to see Wilson on business. I found him like that."

"You're lying. You weren't there to see Anton, because... because..." She hesitated.

I probed a little. "Because you know what his business is?"

The cold mask of her face began to crumple around the eyes and mouth, and then it fell away, leaving a small girl staring out at me in hopeless confusion. She began to cry.

I took her free hand, and guided her to the sofa. As she sat she released the stun gun, which fell in an unheeded clatter to the floor. Now sobbing uncontrollably, she leaned forward, burying her face against my chest. Her body shook from the wracking sobs, and my shirt became wet with her tears.

Finally she was quiet. Then, in a small voice, she said, "He was my brother, my older brother. There are so few of us. I tried to be strong, but—I just couldn't hold it all in."

"When I saw it," I said softly, "I threw up. It's not a sight to keep any Citizen sane."

"Oh, *that*. I don't mean that. I'm not worried about being picked up. But Anton, getting involved like that... and then, dying so horribly...."

"You're not making a lot of sense to me. What was Anton involved in?"

"He—" she broke off. "Just where do you fit in? I've never seen you before, and I know everyone who knows—"

"Let's just leave it that I wandered in. Okay?" I felt very tired. It was nearing the end of a very long day for me. Momentarily my vision blurred and doubled, and there were two Barbara Wilsons sitting close to me on the couch. I climbed wearily to my feet.

"Now that you've brought me here, what next? Shouldn't you be reporting me to the proctors if you're going to keep on thinking I killed him? Or—have you your own reason for avoiding them?"

Her voice seemed to echo distantly in my ears. "I don't know, I just don't know. I thought picking you up was the right thing at the time, but now... I think we'd better wait for Norman. He's the one who phoned. He's—"

She was staring at me strangely now. I felt my body numbing, my mouth starting to gape open.

"*Run!*" I choked, and struggled to close my mouth.

She snatched the stun gun from beside her, raised it, and fired it at me. I felt a distant tingling in my nerves, a pins-and-needles feeling—nothing else. I cried with silent despair. A thin red beam carved her apart, while her hand still held down the button on the stun gun.

It was as before. The deed done, I was free. I could feel my muscles unlocking, as though from cramps. I fell drunkenly to the floor.

When I came to it was dark in the big room, the last cherry embers of dusk dying in the west. Slowly I picked myself up, and went to the couch.

In death she looked young, much younger. Her features had relaxed, carried with them the innocence of sleep. She looked barely sixteen. If you didn't stare down at her charred and bloodied bodice, you would never know she hadn't simply drifted off into pleasant, childlike dreams. I reached out my hand and touched her hair, fingering it gently. It had a light fragrance, smelled freshly washed. I dropped my hand and let it slide down the smooth curve of her cheek.

Her skin was cold and strangely unresilient. She was dead. I had killed her. I felt the moisture on my cheeks, but could not feel myself crying. Finally I straightened up, and left the room.

I looked at myself in the bathroom mirror for a long time. I stared myself in the eyes, trying to see past their gray irises. I looked at my close-cropped, nondescript reddish-brown hair, at the faint lines developing in my forehead, and around my eyes.

Then I turned, and with all the force I could put into it, I threw my fist into the wall.

The old ceramic tiles shattered, plaster dust raining down upon the floor with their clattering remnants, and I stared at my hand. I'd felt nothing break. There had been the first flash of pain which traveled up my arm, and the solid driving feel of my knuckles grinding into the old and brittle tiles. But there was no real pain afterwards. My knuckles were raw and red, bits of tile and plaster imbedded in the open, bleeding flesh. But they didn't hurt any longer.

I started the water running in the wash basin, washed off my hand. I could feel the tingling of the water on my lacerations, and its coldness had started to numb my fingers before I turned the water off.

I sat down on the rim of the bathtub, and let my hand lie in my lap. The light in the white-tiled room was bright. I stared closely at the back of my hand.

The blood had started clotting almost as soon as I'd taken my hand out of the water. Now it had formed a series of hard scabs. It was a dark brown, and looked old. Underneath it, my knuckles itched slightly.

I sat and stared at my hand for half an hour, my mind numb. Then I rose, flexing my hand, returned to the wash basin, and began picking the scabs off with my other hand.

Two—the ones covering the knuckles I'd laid open the worst—didn't want to come off yet. The others peeled off readily, exposing bright pink scar tissue underneath.

I opened my mouth, and tried to angle myself in such a position that I could stare into the back of my mouth. It was impossible. The light was wrong, and the angles were wrong. With my left hand I reached into my mouth and tried to probe the back of it. I could feel nothing with my finger, but moments later I was doubled over the basin retching. Not much was left to come up.

It didn't seem like a very hard idea for a sane Citizen to get used to: I was a well constructed machine, camouflaged to look human—even to myself—and designed to commit murder.

I picked up the stun gun from where it'd fallen by her open hand. "Well," I said, too loudly, "now you know how it happened to Anton."

The phone rang. The shrill jangle slashed across my nerves, and I jumped. I started towards it, and then stopped. The phone kept on ringing. After the twelfth ring, I couldn't stand it. It was going to ring all night. I lifted the phone off the hook momentarily, then dropped it again. The bell was stilled.

I hated to do it, but there was still one task left. I had to find her personal things and go through them.

She'd carried no purse, but she must've had an ID on her. One can't get anywhere or do anything without an ID. Ever since currency was abolished, the ID permanent credit card has been the sole purchasing agent. For anything from a phone call to subway tokens to a dinner out, your card in a slot pays the tab. The magnetic code strip on the bottom edge of the plastic card not only keys in the accounting system of the computer-complex to deduct the current tab from your account, but also will trigger a reject if your account is flat at the moment. It's a handy way of keeping the Citizenry under sane control....

Barbara's clothing was close-fitting; I felt uncomfortable as I searched for a pocket that might hold a small wallet or even an ID. Finally, I was forced to the conclusion that she didn't have one on her. But surely there was one somewhere in the house. I started for the back of the apartment.

There was a faint scraping noise in the hall, then the muffled metallic jangle of keys. I pulled the stun gun from where I'd stuck it in my belt, and moved behind the door.

The lock turned over in a barely audible click. Whoever it was was being quite cautious. I waited in silence as the door swung open, masking me from the person on the other side.

He was attracted by the light streaming into the entryway through the dining room from the front room beyond. He took several steps inside, and had reached behind him to close the door, when he saw her body on the sofa under the windows. With a grunt, he gave the door a swing, and started towards the light. Then something made him cautious again. As the door thudded shut, he pivoted, facing me.

I raised my hand with the stun gun in it, pointing it at him. "Okay," I said, "stop right there. Who are you?"

With the light behind him, it was difficult to make out his features, but he was of medium height, and very thick. His shoulders were impossibly broad, his torso a barrel. His legs seemed too short for the rest of him. His close-cropped hair stood up in rusty spikes.

"The name is Edwards. Norman Edwards. And who might you be?"

"I'm the man with the stun gun. We'll let the name go for a while. Who are you to her?" I gestured with the gun at the room behind him.

"Is—is she—?"

"Barbara is dead," I said. "I was here. I saw it happen. There was nothing I could do to stop it. You haven't answered my question."

"She's my cousin." He turned, and without another word went into the front room. I followed, at a safe distance. He looked like a man who could make himself dangerous.

He stared down at her for a long moment, then knelt beside her, and took her hand. "I'll get the bastard for you," he said softly. "I'll fix him." Then he stood again.

"You saw him do it? You saw who it was?"

I regretted my earlier statement. "I didn't see him, no. But—"

"What do you mean, you didn't see him?" Edwards' features twisted into a heavy scowl, his eyebrows drawing together. "You just said you saw it happen!"

"I meant I saw her get it. Somebody opened the door and shot her with a laser ray. By the time I got there, he was gone."

"Yeah?" His voice was doubting. "A laser is a stupid thing to use as a weapon. You need a power source, power lines, a lot of delicate equipment. That's not the sort of thing you can go sneaking up with and take potshots with."

"Okay, have it your way. I did it to her with this stun gun."

He balled a fist, and raised it. I hefted the gun slightly, and he shrugged. "Okay," he said. "Okay, that's the way you saw it, that's the way it happened—maybe."

"Isn't it about time we called the proctors?" I asked.

Edwards was kneeling again by Barbara's side. This time he was more interested in her wound. "The proctors? I don't think so. I don't think you'd be too anxious to have them come, yourself. She's been dead for some time—the blood's dried. You've had plenty of time to call them. No, I don't think you want them any more than I do. By the way, where'd you get one of their guns?"

# V

My knuckles itched where the scabs still held. I was clenching the gun too tightly in my fist. My thumb was drawn towards the small button that would knock this quarrelsome anthropoid unconscious and leave me free to exit. I didn't hear anyone else come into the apartment.

"He got it from me," said a familiar voice.

I stumbled, my thumb involuntarily mashing down on the trigger button, as I whirled in surprise. Behind me I heard the heavy thump of Edwards' body on the floor.

"You! By sanity, you gave me a shock. Don't *do* that!"

Hoyden laughed. "I gave you a shock? Look at poor Norman!"

I'd hit him in the leg. He was doubled up, lying on his side, clenching his leg. His leg was kicking spasmodically.

Hoyden said, "You only hit him a glancing blow, but you've given him a king-sized cramp."

Grunting from the exertion, I lifted the smaller, but heavier man to his feet. "Walk on it," I told him. "That's the only way."

He nodded, his lips drawn back over his teeth in a snarling grimace, and began hobbling around the room. Slowly his leg straightened and he paced more normally, with only a slight limp.

Hoyden had quickly sobered. "I'm sorry, Norman. If I'd known the effect I was going to have on our jumpy friend, I wouldn't have been so quiet about it."

"Sneaky, I calls it," I said, forcing a weak laugh. We were all friends here now. But I kept a good grip on the stun gun dangling at my side.

Edwards joined the spirit of the occasion, and said, in a rueful tone of voice, "I guess I should be glad you only nicked me." Then his simian face grew heavy again and he said, "But that gets us back to where we were. Why'd you give him the gun, Hoyden?"

It was a good question. I wondered about the answer to that one myself.

"For his protection," she said smoothly. "Daddy is after him. They had him up in one of the special wards at Bellevue. I got him out, gave him the gun, and told him to come here. I thought he'd be safe with Barbara. Where *is* Barbara, by the way?"

Edwards' face loosened, and his brows fell. "You—you didn't—?" He gestured at the couch.

It was Hoyden's first awareness that something had happened to Barbara. Somehow, in the preceding melee, she'd completely missed the pathetic form under the now black windows. Her face grew taut, her skin etched with thin, pink lines vivid against her sudden pallor. For a few moments she looked ageless and aged. Then her mouth seemed to twist, and she shot me an intense look that I could not decipher. But she said only one word.

*"Daddy."*

"It appears she was killed by a laser beam," Edwards said.

As if she'd not heard him, Hoyden focused her full attention upon me. "I think we'd better be going now," she said, her voice as taut as her face, the tone giving the words a strange emphasis. Then she turned on her heel, and headed for the door.

I hesitated for a moment, and looked at Edwards. He gave me a shrouded look and glanced away. I shrugged, and followed Hoyden.

Without a glance over her shoulder, Hoyden strode out into the hall, and then turned for the stairs leading up. I followed, dumbly, wondering what I was getting myself into now. It seemed easier for the moment to ride on inertia and leave the initiative to someone else—someone who at least appeared to have some of the answers.

At first I thought we were climbing for one of the upper floors, but as we rounded the last turn of stairs, I saw we'd come to a hall, the end of which opened onto the roof.

Hoyden stepped through the door, and I followed her out onto the gummy, tarpapered roof, and around to the side where I could see, highlights gleaming in stray reflections from nearby apartment windows, a small hovercraft.

Once, it seemed to me when I was quite young, I was in a library and had a chance to browse through an ancient set of encyclopedias. In one volume predictions were made about the future. It was very amusing to me to see how badly these amateur Nostradamuses had prophesied. They envisioned strange automobiles with high narrow bodies that looked like overturned canoes and almost detached, but very streamlined, pontoon fenders. They imagined the cities of my century would have great elevated speedway ramps entwining about sleek skyscrapers that pointed skyward like rocket-ships, and in the sky and in the upper reaches of the cities' canyons would move vast orderly streams of helicopters as thick as the traffic in Manhattan's streets had been before the Ban.

They overlooked the fact that any city of size is never going to tear all its buildings down and rebuild them from the ground up, at one point in time, and to uniform architectural design. Our cars, low, flat, wedge shaped, although I'd not seen many because of my infrequent trips to the outlying boroughs, certainly bore little resemblance to those I'd seen pictured. And the thought of congested streams of helicopters, even in their present-day sophistication, would move the average Citizen to horror.

It's been said that the twenty-first century has progressed far more slowly than the twentieth—that, indeed, all our major innovations and developments date back into the 1900's, but nonetheless our progress has been sane and orderly, not helter-skelter. The sole aircraft allowed in thickly populated areas is one of several variations of the GEM—the Ground Effect Machine.

The hovercraft is the most common. It is a stable platform which floats, normally, on a two- to six-inch cushion of air, generated by fans within the body. It can skim over any surface, even water. Over the platform there is a passenger compartment, usually with two or four seats. The hovercraft is designed so that it can reach altitudes of forty to a hundred feet, for short hops, enabling those few who possess them to park them on roofs and jump over trees. I'd never ridden in one before; only the higher-level administrators owned them.

Hoyden's was a two-seater coupe design, but mounted on a platform that struck me as unusually large. The basic shape of the platform was a blunted oblong, with ducts over fans mounted fore and aft, the passenger compartment a plexiglass bulge in the center. Hoyden swung out a door at the side, and scrambled in, and over to the seat on the opposite side. I followed her in gingerly, climbing up onto the step on the platform, and then awkwardly sticking one foot into the compartment, pivoting, almost losing my balance, and then sitting down suddenly in the too-low seat and somehow pulling my other leg in. I started to reach for the door, but she pushed a button and it clamped solidly shut, my ears popping slightly. I felt a fool.

There were controls in front of each seat, but I sat back and watched her as she leaned forward, mouth still set with grim determination, and flipped on the motor switch.

The instrument lights came on, and there was a faint humming and an almost imperceptible vibration. I tried to relax in my contoured seat. Then she threw in the clutch, and a low moaning began, which quickly ascended the scale into a muted scream. I glanced out the window next to me, and saw a roof seam slip quietly by. We were already airborne — floating on air. As we moved towards the roof's edge, I saw dust and grit jet out to the sides. My knuckles were itching again.

Then we were at the edge. I strained forward. There was nothing in front of us but the topmost branches of a tree across the way, waving in our headlights.

We hung, poised at the end of the roof, for what seemed an eternity. Then Hoyden slammed her foot on a pedal and the whine leapt to a banshee scream of defiance, and we were out over Fifth Avenue, four flights up, and jetting downtown.

Since the flight was through darkness, I quickly lost track of my bearings. Familiar landmarks looked totally alien from the air, and as soon as we headed across the East River, the fans muted again and the water so close it looked like it would wash over us, I was completely lost, my only landmarks in the other boroughs of the city the subway stations.

Once beyond the river, we made a couple of jumps and settled down onto a road — an expressway, actually — and joined its traffic. It was difficult to tell, since all I could make out were blinding headlights and winking taillights, but apparently the traffic was equally divided between hovercrafts and wheeled cars.

From time to time I would glance at Hoyden, but the blue light from the instrument panel revealed her expression to be unchanged; she was in no mood for conversation.

After some time, we swung off from the anonymity of the featureless expressway, and down onto a local street.

From the expressway signs, I gathered we were in Brooklyn. I'd been in Brooklyn only rarely — my attitude towards the other boroughs as provincial as most Manhattanites' — and the sight of the archaic streets, filled with lumbering buses, darting cars, and gliding hovercrafts was still a fresh experience for me.

We appeared to be in one of the poorer districts. People crowded the sidewalks, not with any purposeful movement, but loitering about storefronts and house stoops, idling on street corners in clusters, and paying no overt attention to those of us driving past.

Few of the cars seemed to stop on these streets, except for momentary pauses at traffic signals. At one such stop, I glanced out to my side, and for a brief moment locked eyes with a flashily-dressed woman on the sidewalk. She was well into her middle age, but dressed a rebellious seventeen. Her hair was bleached almost white, and the powerful mercury-vapor light overhead gave it a bluish hue. The same light made her too-tight red dress a ghastly harsh color. It did nothing for her make-up, either, her heavily painted lips a gaping black hole in the unhealthy pastry of her face. Twin spots of rouge on her cheeks were picked out like great moles. My feelings must've shown in my expression, for her gaze of sullen curiosity turned suddenly to an intense look of hatred. Then she swiveled to greet a man on the sidewalk, took his arm, and directed him for the dingy doorway directly opposite. Over it hung a neon sign that hissed and flickered. *Rooms – Transients* it said. Then we were moving again.

Gradually the neighborhood changed, the sidewalks grew emptier, until we were in a warehouse district, and the cobbled streets were empty, even of other vehicles. We came to a floating stop, finally, in an alleyway before the large and rust-flaked doors of an apparently abandoned building.

Hoyden pushed another button, and one of the doors slid silently open. As we glided in past it, I saw that it ran on a well-oiled inner track.

Then we were in a great barn-like room, the ceiling stretching high above us into darkness, our headlights picking out a gray and crumbling concrete floor which faded away beyond our lights. Hoyden swung us to the right, along the wall we'd entered through. Our lights seized upon and held a flight of metal-shod stairs that climbed along the wall. We stopped at their bottom, the fans dropping to a whisper, and a light jar signaling that we were once more in solid contact with terra firma.

Hoyden fumbled for a moment under her seat, and then withdrew a black cylinder. A beam of light sprang from it as she cut the hovercraft's lights. There was a slight click, and my door was open. Feeling like a gawky adolescent who'd not yet grown accustomed to his new stature, I maneuvered myself out of the seat and the hovercraft.

Hoyden had exited on her own side, and was standing beside me by the time I was out and on my feet again. "Up," she said, tersely, her flashlight beam pointing the way.

The stairs had lost interest in their duty over the passing of the years; now they sagged down, away from the wall, at a dangerous angle. There was no handrail. I hesitated at their foot, and, with a faint contemptuous sound, she pushed past me and began mounting the steps two at a time.

As I followed her up, the sole illumination bobbing ahead of us and darkness closing in behind and below, a detached part of my mind, with a supreme disregard for the occasion and the events of the past day, was fixed appreciatively upon the well-limned figure she presented me. She was wearing trousers as snug and close-fitting as those Barbara'd had on—I wrenched my mind away from Barbara. Her brother was only a dead cipher to me, but she would always be far more.

Then Hoyden's light was bouncing upon a door, and we were on a small enclosed landing. Grotesque shadows danced about us as she fumbled with the door, shifting her light from one hand to the crook of the other arm, keys jangling in her other hand. She leaned forward, then straightened, triumphantly. There was a solid click of a bolt being turned, and then the door opened.

As she entered, she reached for a light switch on the wall to her right, and the room leaped into being.

It was like stepping from one world into another. Outside, closed from us now by a scarred, metal-faced door, was a vast and empty warehouse. Here was an apartment furnished with an opulence I'd never seen before.

We were standing on a rich, thick rug, patterned in designs of orange, rust, and sienna. My shoes did not quite sink out of sight in it. We were in a sort of anteroom, a wing off the main room visible beyond. On the neutral beige walls to my right and left hung paintings. One was huge—it covered most of the wall—and seemed to be the work of one of those already condemned, great splatters of color romping across it in utter chaos. The other was smaller, but more intense, slashes of violent reds and blacks on a white background that seemed to be showing me something, if only I could grasp it.

I followed Hoyden reluctantly into the main room. The furniture was low, spare, and yet richly inviting. Polished wood curved beckoningly, revealing warm foam cushions as a Venus flytrap displays its lures to trap helpless insects. A low planter served as a room-divider, real ivy caressing its bricks. Hoyden moved around it, to a long, low bar on its other side.

I stood and watched her as she reached under it for a bottle, and poured from it into two short glasses. Then she came back to where I stood, and handed me my drink.

I accepted it numbly, and did nothing.

"Drink. Go on, drink it, you big dummy," she said.

"What is it?" I asked.

"Whiskey," she replied. At the blank look on my face, she elaborated. "Jack Daniels, Green Label, charcoal filtered. Very smooth." She tossed down most of hers and repeated, in a huskier voice, "Smo-o-o-oth..."

I tasted it. It nipped my tongue, and slipped down my throat like greased fire.

"Ahh," I said, "it's, ummm—"

"Alcohol. You've heard of it?"

I had, but I'd never tasted it before. One of the first acts of the sane state was to outlaw drugs which could make the mind unstable. I took another sip. This time the jolt hit me in the stomach, expanding into a small nova. It reminded me that my last meal had been long ago. I took another drink. I could see why they'd outlawed the stuff.

"Very interesting," I said, staring down at my empty glass. Its bottom seemed a long way off.

"Let me get you some more," Hoyden said, easing the glass from my grip, and taking it back to the bar. I had to admire the way she moved: all litheness and grace, like a feline. Feeling taller and clumsier than usual, I followed her around the bar. Her hair curved down around her cheek, as she leaned over to pour. She looked beautiful.

"You look beautiful," I heard someone say. I looked around, but there was no one behind me. When I turned back to her, she was holding my glass out to me, and laughing.

"My, this stuff must work on you, after all," she said.

My fingers felt a little fuzzy as I took hold of the glass, and I almost spilled the drink trying to see what would make them feel that way. The problem bothered me—if I wasn't going to spill the drink, I'd have to do something else with it. Nonchalantly, I threw it down my throat in one fiery gulp.

"Whew!" Hoyden said, in appreciation.

"Huhhhh!" I shuddered, involuntarily. I lifted my hand to about six inches from my eyes, and tried to focus upon it. It was impossible. I moved it farther back. I was a little too abrupt—the glass left my fingers and sailed across the room to smash against the far wall.

"Gee, sorry about that," I said thickly.

"That's all right. I have lots more. Would you like another?" There seemed to be a wicked look in her eyes, but I couldn't be sure.

"I think I'll sit down," I said. "Will they eat me?"

"Huh?" she asked, looking over her shoulder from the bar. "Sure, go ahead. Make yourself at home."

Time seemed to pass in fits and starts. I had hardly seated myself when she was sitting next to me, and a drink was in my hand again. "Flame on!" I said, and drank about half of it. I'd lost connection with my stomach.

Then I had one arm around her shoulder and was gazing soulfully into her eyes and saying, "I don't know what's happening to me. I think I'm insane." And she was patting me gently on the head.

My next lucid moment found me with my head in her lap, gazing up at her face, which was bent down over me. "You look like Barbara," I was saying, "only more beautiful." I had a sudden freezing sensation as I remembered Barbara, and for a moment I was cold sober, adrenalin pumping through my system. My forehead broke into a sweat, and as she let her cool hand soothe the perspiration away, she held a glass to my lips with the other.

"I'm hot," I said, stumbling to my feet. My legs were rubbery and I almost collapsed again. "It's hot in here!" Suddenly she looked like a witch, a vengeful temptress of a witch. I leaned over the couch, and yanked her to her feet, pulling her up and against me. I put my big arms around her, and kissed her, savagely. She did not resist.

# VI

When I woke up, I found myself diagonally angled across a double bed. There was no one else in it.

The sheets were silky smooth to the touch. They were gold satin. There were two pillows, one under my head, the other almost off the bed. Both looked slept-upon, but I couldn't be sure who was responsible.

The room had a feminine look to it. There was a deep pile lilac carpet that stretched to the walls. There was a long dresser along one wall which also doubled for a dressing table. The wall above it was all mirror, straight to the ceiling. The wall opposite the bed had windows, thin draperies hanging in front of them, diffusing the glow of sunlight. There were two doors on the third wall, one of them partly open, and a fragment of the living-room showing beyond it. Between the doors was an easy chair. My clothes—Charles Simpson's clothes, actually—were flung over it in wild disarray. I thought about that for a moment, and checked. Yes, all my clothes. Behind me, I could hear the noise of water running; the door next to the bed must be the bathroom, I surmised.

I flung the sheets off, and swiveled around to a sitting position. I felt fine. Absently, I rubbed my knuckles, and then looked down at them. The scabs were gone, and so was the pink freshness. My knuckles reminded me of yesterday. I stopped feeling so fine.

The water kept right on running in the bathroom, so I climbed off the bed, and walked over to the windows. I wanted a breath of fresh air.

I pushed the drapes aside, but instead of clear glass, I saw rusted frames, many small panes, and each covered over with thin tissue paper through which the sun's rays still strove. The window was permanently closed. It was ugly in comparison with the rest of the room, and suddenly I remembered why. We'd come in through a dilapidated old warehouse last night, and this window was part of it. Obviously, the luxuriously fitted apartment within was not for public knowledge. I remembered the people I'd seen on the streets too, and didn't have to wonder why—only how.

Something was very much wrong. My whole world had been an ordered, sane and sensible world until yesterday. In my world there were only ordered, sane and sensible people who went about their duties with an ordered, sane and sensible monotony. There was no murder—unless you counted the Executions, which were a public duty—no crime, no luxury and no poverty. Deviants were easily picked out by the scanners, and picked up by the proctors.

Everything had been turned topsy-turvy, starting with the execution itself and the strange girl I'd seen there. It seemed to me that I was noticing women for the first time in my life. And that made me think of Hoyden.

The water stopped running.

I had my pants on when she opened the door and came out with a breath of steam surrounding her. She wasn't wearing pants. Or anything else.

We stared at each other for a while. She was worth staring at: a youthful slender body, put together exactly right with no left over pieces. She held herself proudly, almost jauntily, as if to say, "Go ahead and look—I know I'm beautiful." She was, too, and somehow her nudity seemed not at all indecent. While I was staring at her I was also wondering about something. The last I could remember of the night before was putting away the last of that bottle of whiskey. We both still had our clothes on then. What had transpired since?

Then, she laughed. "Well, you certainly look healthy enough!" She glanced beyond me at the window, and winced. "Oooh, that light! I never can stand it when I'm hung over." She opened the other door, and stepped into a closet. A light had gone on inside of it when the door opened, like a refrigerator. A moment later she reappeared, attired in a satin housecoat. "I'm not all that wanton," she said. "I didn't expect you to be awake already. After all I poured into you last night, I thought you'd be good for twelve hours."

"I seem to have a strong constitution," I said, my face blank.

The smile slipped from hers. "That's right; so you do," she said. "But not a perfect one, it seems."

"What happened last night?" I asked.

"You got drunk."

"I know—from all that alcohol. I'm surprised I'm still alive. I thought it was supposed to be toxic."

"I'm not sure anything's toxic on you," she said, enigmatically.

"But that wasn't what I meant. I meant later. What happened?"

She glanced at the bed. "Oh. Oh, we went to bed." She got that slightly wicked look on her face again. "We went straight to bed, without passing Go, and without collecting two hundred dollars." That one slipped completely by me.

"There seem to be some gaps in my memory," I said.

"That's not the only place," she said.

I shook my head. I reached for my shirt, and started to put it on. "You've been having your fun with me since last night. The jokes are wearing a little thin, now. Isn't it about time you started telling me a few things?"

"Like what?"

"Like who you are."

"I thought you knew. You knew my name."

"I found your name—just your first name—inscribed on a photo in a dead man's wallet," I said. "On this." I took the picture from my shirt pocket and gave it to her.

The laughter and defiance was suddenly gone from her face. "Yes, poor Anton. And—and Barbara. That leaves only Arthur in the Wilson family. Daddy's working fast." She looked up from the photo at me. "You really don't know, do you? You poor guy. But there's no use in my telling you—it wouldn't do you any good. It wouldn't do any of us any good."

"For sanity's sake!" I said. "Stop playing games!"

"I've stopped. I won't play games any longer," she said. She reached into the folds of her robe and withdrew my stun gun. "This is necessary," she said. "It's absolutely necessary. It's for your own good and for our good. I'm sorry."

She pressed the button, and I felt the vibrations racing along my nerves. This was no faint tingling as before—it was the real thing. I was numb, and I felt like I was watching TV and the picture was going—blackness grew in from around the edges and I was peering down a telescoping tunnel.

"My full name is Hoyden Nash," she said, her voice barely reaching me before I passed out.

They were right. You do wake up with a terrible hangover. I'd felt nothing from the alcohol—apparently my system could cope with that. But the effects of the dislocating vibrations upon my entire nervous system were far stronger.

I woke up sick to my stomach. I vomited a thin yellow bile that stank faintly of whiskey all down my front and lap. I couldn't help it; I was tied securely in a chair. Not one of those soft modern chairs in her living-room. This one was made of chromed tubes of steel, and the plastic-covered wire that bound me to it was quite strong enough to hold me, especially in my sick and weakened condition.

After my eyes had cleared of their tears and I was able to concentrate on my surroundings, I saw that I was in the bathroom. The chair was probably a kitchen chair, dragged in here for the purpose. She was not a big girl; getting me into the bathroom and onto the chair was probably her limit. I wondered about the reason for the bathroom at first, but then figured it out: it seemed reasonable she knew I might be sick when I woke up. Better on tiled floors than a carpet. She had a practical strain.

She'd done a good job of tying me up, too. My calves and ankles were lashed to the legs of the chair, my arms crossed behind its back and lashed in place, and then, for good measure, my chest and thighs had also been tied down. The plastic covering on the wire kept it from cutting into me badly, but it was still wire, and it had no stretch. My circulation seemed to be gone from my hands and feet. I tried moving my fingers and wriggling my toes without being able to feel a thing.

The bathroom was fitted out on the same luxurious level as the rest of the place. There were two baths, a tub, and a shower stall. The washbowl was more like a separate dressing table, with a bowl set in one end and hardly intruding. The richness of the fittings was far from the Spartan functionality of my own. A practical portion of my mind wondered just where she'd gotten them.

A more immediately concerned part of me wanted to get untied and cleaned up. I had doubts about the first part of that—if she'd tied me up, she probably had a reason—but at least I wanted to stop having to smell that smell of vomit, and get the taste of it out of my mouth. A pill or two for my ringing headache wouldn't hurt either.

"Hoyden! Hey, Hoyden!" It came out a lot more weakly than I intended. I tried again. "Hoyden!" I shouted. My stomach contracted, and a wave of fresh nausea hit me. I wanted to lie down very badly. There were no answering sounds from elsewhere in the apartment. I listened as intently as my buzzing head and leaping stomach would let me. I heard nothing, nothing at all.

The first half hour was the worst. After that, the next two hours went much more easily, except for the smell that I couldn't escape, which tended to restimulate my nausea.

Stun guns work on a very simple principle. They are designed to knock a person unconscious without inflicting any physical damage on him. The proctors, who are selected for their nonviolent attitudes and the unlikelihood of their possibly abusing their positions, have insisted on stun guns. The condemned often become quite violent in resisting detention, and the proctors wanted neither to have to rough them up nor get roughed up themselves. The scientific principle behind the stun gun had been lying about for years—someone had invented the first stun gun to make war "humane." Naturally, any society insane enough to want war won't be sane enough to be humane about it; the stun gun was filed and forgotten in the military files. It wasn't until sanity prevailed, and we began feeding all the accumulated data into the computer-complex (for one thing, just to get rid of all those tons of files), and began getting cross-correlations, that the stun gun popped up again.

Basically the stun gun emits a vibration which attacks the nerve centers of the body. There has to be some fairly fine tuning, or it would simply kill. But that's taken care of in the manufacture of the gun—you can't reset an existing gun because all the components are designed to work at only one frequency. The ultrasonics cause a temporary dislocation in the senses and most of the motor nerves. It's not unlike being knocked out physically, except that there are no bruises, no contusions, lacerations, or concussions. Just a hangover. It seemed a shame they hadn't found a way to eliminate that, too.

Still, I shucked off the hangover faster than might've been expected. I wondered whether I would've had one if I hadn't consumed so much alcohol the night before. Then I remembered the last time I'd been shot with a stun gun. I hadn't been under my own control then. It was becoming very obvious that I was two entirely different people—that when I was under that control I was capable of a great deal that I couldn't manage on my own, like resisting stun guns. But some features carried over, like my extraordinary healing ability.

I had plenty of time to think about these things. After all, I wasn't going anywhere.

After three hours, I gave up speculation as a dead end. I knew what I knew, and that was that. There were others who knew more than I did. I knew that, too. And I knew that sooner or later they'd tell me what they knew, one way or another. That I was very sure of. The memory of a dead girl on a couch made me quite sure.

I started counting the tiles in the floor. They were not arranged in neat rows, but rather in a semi-random pattern that repeated itself roughly every foot. First I tried to isolate the squares that contained each pattern, trying to recognize the lines that separated each of those blocks, the lines where each pattern started over again. Then, once I'd done that within the entire visible area of the floor, I started counting the tiles in one complete block. My aim, I think, was to figure an approximation of the total number of tiles in the floor. But I never got that far.

This time I recognized the effects. It began with a feeling that I was seeing double, that there were two of me, superimposed, and slowly splitting apart. Pretty soon there was only one of me again: imprisoned. The other self—the one in control, in whose body I was a helpless, watching passenger—began to strain against the wires.

If I could've, I would have screamed. Pain lanced through my wrists and arms. I could feel the wires slicing through my skin as my arms strained to break them. Suddenly there was a sharp *crack*, like a rifle report, and wires were snapping loose in front of me. My arms came around in front and I stared at the ripped flesh and flowing blood. While my hands untied the rest of me my clothing became saturated with blood.

There was still no feeling, for me at least, in my feet when I stood up. But my body didn't falter. I left a smear of blood on the door handle when I yanked the bathroom door fully open and strode out into the bedroom, and through into the living-room.

I was almost to the entryway when the outer door opened. Hoyden pushed in through it, and then stopped.

I stopped and faced her, my slashed arms hanging at my sides. The blood was coagulating now. It had stopped dripping.

The color drained from her face, very much as it had when she'd seen Barbara. *"Daddy, no!"* she said. I said nothing. "I won't let you," she said in a breathless voice. "I tried to stop you — I tied him up. You've got to stop. *You'll have to kill me too."*

Suddenly I strode forward, raised one arm, and knocked her aside. Before I'd gotten through the door I'd seen the smear of blood on her face, and knew my arm was bleeding again. But Daddy didn't care.

The cavernous warehouse below was vaguely streaked with light that poked half-heartedly through boarded-over windows. As I moved down the trembling stairs, I felt my metabolism speeding up. By the time I reached the bottom, I was hurtling three steps at a time.

*"No!"* came the cry at the top of the stairs. I felt a faint tingle and knew she was using the stun gun. But that was worse than useless — I was out of its effective range anyway.

The catches on the hovercraft's doors seemed to be giving me trouble. My hands were fumbling them without success. They were becoming smeared with brown stains.

Then there was a click, and a pneumatic sigh from the door mechanism, and it sprang back. Behind me I heard an explosion.

Something slapped the crumbling concrete at my feet and skeetered away with a high-pitched whine. Then there was a second explosion, and something gave my pants leg a sharp tug and almost simultaneously there was a *sprang* from the metal body of the hovercraft and a small hole appeared right in front of me.

The thing was as hard to get into as before. I was pulling my left leg in when I heard a third shot, and a hot fire lanced through my thigh.

My body didn't pause. The door slammed, and the motor, already running, engaged the fan, and I was moving. There were no more shots. My head was held up, watching the progress of the hovercraft, so I could not see my leg, but I could feel my bloody pants caking against it.

The trip was an absolute nightmare. While one part of me—the "I" who thought and felt—looked on in a stunned state of near shock, tumbled thoughts of being shot at with illegal, explosively propelled bullets, of the ceaseless slaughter and carnage of which I was being forced to become part, all coursing through my mind—another part of me was coolly and efficiently guiding the hovercraft through a maze of streets I'd never traveled before, and doing so as though the drive were an everyday occurrence.

Now we were heading along narrow, tree-shaded streets. As we turned a corner I had a glimpse of a short block ending with a railing and a few park benches, and beyond that a view of lower Manhattan across the water. We were in Brooklyn Heights, then. It was one of the few neighborhoods I had any familiarity with outside Manhattan.

It was apparently early afternoon. There were few people on the streets. The hovercraft stopped before a brownstone. I'd been dividing my attention between my surroundings and the way my body'd been handling the hovercraft—it seemed like knowing how to run one might be a handy thing.

When I climbed out, I felt the caked blood on my pants leg pull loose, and new blood trickle down my leg. But, as with my torn arms, there was no longer any pain. Only an itching ache.

As I went down a few steps to the entrance of the building, I noticed the number over the door was Forty-one. It didn't tell me anything. Inside was a foyer. The inner door was locked. Without hesitation my fist smashed through the opaque glass in the door, and I unlocked it from the inside. Then things were speeding up again and I was bounding up the carpet-covered stairs.

I climbed three flights to the top floor. The hall was awash with sunshine from the skylight. A fly was circling about in a lazy drone. I leaned back against the hall railing and kicked with both feet against the apartment door.

Daddy was getting clumsy. The railing collapsed, as I drove backwards to slam against the wall and then dropped down the stairwell. But it didn't matter. Almost immediately I had vaulted up into the hall again and hit the door with my shoulder. This time it gave, part of the inner frame tearing away in a curtain of plaster and splintered wood.

As I came through the door I saw no one, but by now my speed was way up, and I heard something to my left, behind the door. I jumped and turned, surprising a tall, thin man in the act of swinging a piece of two-by-four at me.

That was it; it was all over then. The board came down on my left shoulder as the beam from my mouth carved into his guts. A moment later he was dead on the floor.

# VII

I woke up between satin sheets.

For a long time I just lay there, my body still drowsing, my mind free-associating between dreams and reality. I was in a bedroom, a feminine bedroom. I knew I'd been there before, and there were the dreams....

I shifted a little, and my muscles in my arms and legs felt stiff, protesting. There seemed to be something wrapped around them.

I sat bolt upright, the golden sheets tumbling away from me. Both my arms were bandaged from wrist to armpit. My left thigh was similarly dressed. I had nothing else on. If it had not been for the bandages, and a few other discrepancies, like the dim light in the room, which crept in through the half-opened door to the living-room and not from the draped windows, I might have thought I was just waking again from a night of drinking with Hoyden.

The door swung wider, and a soft form was silhouetted in the doorway. "You're awake?"

She came into the room. She was dressed in a loose, diaphanous gown which did not mask the natural curves of her body from the light behind her. Her hair was caught back in a ribbon. She wasn't wearing her glasses. Only her face belied the seductive picture she presented. It was tired and empty.

"You came after me?" I asked.

"Yes," dully.

"You got me out of there—down all those stairs and into the hovercraft, bloody and filthy all over—after, after…?"

"After you killed Arthur Wilson. Yes. Yes, I did that."

She sat down on the foot of the bed. "Why?" I asked.

She shook her head. "I don't know. I really don't know. If—if it hadn't been for last night… I wouldn't have. It wouldn't have mattered to me. But, well, I guess I just decided you deserved a chance too. As much as they'll have, which isn't much."

"Hoyden," I said. I reached out to her, and, cupping her chin in my hand, I lifted her face up. I stared into her eyes. "Hoyden, what's going on? Tell me; you know."

"You—you're just a pawn. You haven't—I don't even know your real name! You don't count! You're just a machine—a murder machine!

"You're not human, you're a robot. You don't have any right to bleed, and sleep and get drunk, and—and—" She broke off into sobs.

Without thinking, I put my arms around her, pulled her closer. She flinched, momentarily, at the touch of my arms, then snuggled closer.

I stared down at the part in her hair, her reddish hair. The Wilsons, Edwards—all had red hair. I stroked her hair gently, my fingers sliding down through her hair to the nape of her neck, up her neck around her ears, tracing along her jaw line to her chin. She tilted her face up, her eyes glistening with tears, her expression softened, her face very young.

"Who *are* you?" she asked. And then she lifted her lips and I kissed her.

It started as a tentative brushing of lips, lips which responded to each other more and more warmly, until I found myself clasping her to me in a strong embrace.

Then we lost our balance, and fell sprawling on the bed, our bodies still locked together.

I stroked her hair and her shoulders gently while she nibbled at my ear. She sighed, contentedly, a warm shudder rippling down her body.

"I don't even know your name," she said, softly.

"Bob Tanner," I said. "How do you do, Miss Nash?"

She stiffened momentarily. "You were still conscious then?"

"Only barely."

"I'm sorry. I shouldn't have tied you up. I didn't realize..."

"I know. You wanted to stop—the murders. Is that why you brought me here in the first place?"

"Yes. Yes, I didn't know what I could do, but I thought, if I could just get you drunk and keep you that way, or—"

My arms itched, intolerably. I rolled away from her and sat up. I started unwinding the gauze from my left arm.

Hoyden watched, eyes wide. "Should—should you be doing that yet?"

I didn't answer. The gauze had soaked up what blood hadn't already dried. Bits of scabs and dried blood flaked off with it. As soon as I had the bandage off, I began scratching, my nails catching and tearing loose the remaining scabs. Hoyden gave an involuntary gasp of surprise. The wounds were gone.

It felt good to scratch. But my right arm still itched. I removed its bandages and scratched it too.

"Every time I start to think of you as—as human—" her voice broke.

"Hoyden," I said, my voice chilled, *"what am I?* You know; tell me!"

"I—I don't know. I know what you were *supposed* to be. You were supposed to be just a—a robot. You weren't supposed to act like a real person, or think like one, or have feelings, or, or be able to make love. Now, now I don't know what to think! I don't know *what* you are." Her full, ripe lower lip was quivering, and a tear slowly separated itself from one eye and moistened its way down her cheek.

"Don't cry, Hoyden," I said, softly. I brushed the tear away, and another appeared in its place. We fell back down onto the bed, next to each other, and I cuddled her, held her close.

After a long time, she spoke again in a small voice.

"When I was a young girl, I used to imagine myself living in elaborate fantasy worlds. The world of sanity and civilization is so very sterile for a girl with an imagination who dreams of bright colors and rich experiences. I read my father's books. He had a great many—a huge private library safe from the proctors. I spent most of my childhood reading his books and imagining I was living within their pages.

"After a while I created a fantasy world of my very own—I nursed it throughout most of my adolescence."

"Tell me about it," I prompted.

"You'll laugh."

"No, I won't." I meant that—I wanted to know her and understand her too well to laugh at her, even if she was completely and outrageously foolish in her fantasies.

"I imagined an empire set in a sort of never-never old China," she said. "Very elaborate customs, civilized, cultured, but with grace, and none of the stiffness of our so-called sanity. I was a princess.... You *are* laughing at me." She pouted at me.

"Well," I said, no longer able to hold a straight face, "maybe you could tell me: in your kingdom was it true what they said about Chinese women?" And then I dodged her fist, grabbed her arm and kissed her. It was a rather lingering kiss.

"All right—have your jokes," she said, pulling away at last. "But it was very real to me then. Much more real than the drab world we really live in.

"I forgot about it when I grew older and discovered boys, and life outside the books. But now—I wish I could go back. I wish I could simply wipe out everything that's been happening. I wish I could just blank out the whole terrible, crazy world and be a Chinese princess and live in a paper world again."

There was, nothing I could say. I held her, and stroked her gently.

"What about you? What was your childhood like? When did you discover the whole mockery of the 'sane world'?"

I tried to answer that. "I—I don't know. I remember when I was a kid, but very indistinctly. I can't seem to remember how I felt then. In fact, I don't really remember growing up that well."

A throbbing began in my temples. I ignored it and tried to concentrate. "That's funny," I muttered.

"What?" she asked.

I put my hands to my head to forestall the growing migraine. "I—I can't seem to get any specific memories."

"Have you ever tried before?"

"What? To remember things? Who needs to remember his childhood? I—I *must* have had one." White flashes seemed to come before my eyes.

"What's happening?" Hoyden asked, concerned.

"My—my memories! I'm losing them! I can't remember! I don't seem to have any memories beyond just a few months ago!"

I struggled out of the bed, and to my feet. *"My god, my god!"* I heard my voice screaming, the edge of it slicing new wounds in my skull.

I lost awareness of Hoyden, of the room. I was caught in a whirlpool of throbbing pain, of almost stroboscopic flashes of intense light. I felt simultaneously as though I was losing my sanity—and finally finding my identity. As though all my sensory impressions had been crossed, shorted out—and beyond the level of reality I'd always accepted, I was on the threshold of a new, more significant reality.

Suddenly I was sitting on the floor, on that thick lilac carpet, water cascading down me and streaking the rug around me. I blinked, shook my head, and stared up at Hoyden, who stood poised with another pitcher full of water in her hand.

I held up my hand. "That's—enough," I sputtered.

"Are you all right?" she asked.

"It's okay," I said. "I know, now." A strange look passed over her face, guarded, afraid.

"I never *was* a child," I said, my voice grinding through the fallen panels of false memories. "After all, how could I be? I'm a construct, a robot—you said it yourself. My bones are metal, my skin and flesh just camouflage, grafted on. There's a laser set into my skull, that fires through my mouth. Who am I to be talking about childhood? How could I ever have been a child? Metal doesn't grow—children aren't born like me!"

I climbed to my feet.

"Hoyden," I asked, "you knew who was to be the third victim, didn't you?"

"I couldn't be sure, but—yes, I thought it would be Arthur Wilson. He was the only Wilson left."

*"Are there more?"*

She wouldn't look at me. "Yes. Yes, there are more."

"Who? How many?"

"I don't know. I wish I knew. I wish I knew where it is going to stop. There are three other families besides ours: the Edwardses, the Flemings, and the Dodges."

"What can we do? Can you warn them?"

"They already know. That won't help them now. I don't know what we can do. At first I thought it would be so simple. I'd just do something to put you out of the way, and that would be enough. Now—"

"Now, I think it's time you told me about Daddy," I said.

"Daddy?"

"Daddy."

She turned away from me, and I seized her shoulders roughly, and jerked her back around to face me.

"It all boils down to Daddy," I said. "It all boils down to the person who turns me into an assassin. Somebody wants them dead. Somebody takes over control of me, and kills them. You know that. You know who it is. You've known all along." Each sentence seemed to slap her in the face. *"Who is Daddy?"* I asked.

"I—I can't tell you."

"You can't? Or you won't?"

"He's my father. I just can't betray him."

*"I see.* You'd rather betray these others—these other families you mentioned. They don't count?"

"No, no, *no!* Oh, I don't know what to do."

"There's one very simple solution. If you won't stop Daddy, you'll have to disarm him." I paused to let that sink in. But before she could answer, I said, "You'll have to kill me."

She stared at me in mute horror. "Kill you? I can't. I'm not even sure I could. I even tried, earlier, with a gun. But now I—"

"It's Daddy or me," I said. "And putting me out of commission is strictly a temporary measure. If he wants these people dead, he'll find other ways."

I shook the last water from my hair. "Is there anything for me to wear?" I asked. The clothes I'd borrowed from Charles Simpson—was it only yesterday?—were obviously fit only for the disposal.

"What are you going to do?"

"I can't force you, Hoyden. If you won't help me, I'll have to do the job on my own."

She smiled a weak smile. "Dressed like that?"

I stared at her, without expression.

"All right," she said. "I can go out and get you some."

I wondered if I really needed to eat. There was obviously a power source within me somewhere for the laser. I hadn't eaten for a long time. Maybe it powered me, too. But then again, habit is a powerful thing, and I felt hungry. While Hoyden was out shopping for clothes for me, I prowled her kitchen, found a freezer under one counter top, and popped a breast of capon with wine sauce into the infraheater. I also dug up a can of orange juice concentrate, and made myself some juice. It burned like strong acid all the way down.

The food was good, though, and although it was probably my imagination, I could almost feel it beginning to rebuild my worn body within seconds after I began eating it. My mood cheered considerably, and I could almost forget the whole successive trauma of the previous two days. I suppressed all speculation over the situation, and instead let my mind dwell pleasantly upon the hour Hoyden and I had spent making love together. I was fairly convinced it was my first such experience with a woman, although I had felt no unfamiliarity in it. I seemed well stocked with generalized memories designed to guide me through almost any social situation without any specific reference to a previous experience. But that line of contemplation led dangerously into the proscribed area of speculation. I let my thoughts return to Hoyden.

There seemed to be two levels to her. On one level she related to me as a person, indeed, as a lover. This was a level of what I could only think of as normality. It was the common, boy-girl chemistry in action, the first sparks kindled the night she'd gotten me drunk. But on the second level stood the reality of our situation: the grim fact that I was a robot committing murders at the bidding of her father. This was an overtone which always, inevitably, intruded between us, even in our moments of freest intimacy. What love existed between us would remain embryonic as long as this situation dominated.

When I'd finished eating, I threw the dishes into the disposal and began hunting for a phone.

Infomat carried no listings for Nash other than that for Miss Hoyden Nash, which I knew. Two things puzzled me: that Daddy Nash would have an unlisted phone—and that there were no other Nashes in the greater New York metropolitan area. It seemed more than ominous. Norman Edwards had a listing, though. On Staten Island.

I thought about that for a moment. I'd been heading for Staten Island, back before—the first murder. Was it still possible? Could I get away? Beyond the puppet-master's influence? Somehow I doubted it. The answer was not to run away from him, but to find him.

Hoyden took me in the hovercraft to the nearest subway station. We passed between rows of shabby warehouse buildings, the streets cobblestoned and rutted. Some had old and rusted railroad tracks set in them, occasional spur lines branching off into the gloom of the warehouse alleys beyond the penetration of the mercury-vapor lights. It was night again and there was no traffic on these streets. The hovercraft's ventilation system drew in the odors of dead fish and salt that always characterize the waterfront and I knew that beyond these hulking shapes must be the piers of the Brooklyn harbor front.

Then we turned and began to leave the warehouses. We crossed a shabby avenue, its sidewalks spotted with litter, cars parked along it in various stages of disembowelment.

"I still don't understand," I said. "How, in a world as ordered and sane as ours, these sort of conditions can exist. I thought they went out with the last century."

Her voice sounded cynical. "Sanity is largely in the minds of the beholders. Do you honestly think that they could clean up all this, in only a few decades? Or that they even want to? This isn't Manhattan, Bob."

Then we were crossing another avenue, this one huddled under a squat, elevated expressway. Even in daylight, this street would be in shadow. Somehow the neon lights over the stores seemed dimmed and uncertain in recognition of their vain task.

At the next avenue, Hoyden pulled in to the curb. "This is Fourth Avenue. The subway's right down there. It'll take you to

Manhattan, and—wherever you're going." Her voice faltered, losing its veneer of briskness.

I leaned towards her, and pulled her face around. "Goodbye, Hoyden," I said. I kissed her. "I love you." Then I flipped the door release, and climbed out.

I stood on the curb, watching, as the door slammed pneumatically into place, and I stared down through the plexiglass, trying to catch something of her expression. It was impossible. The light turned green, and with a faint whoop, and an eddy of dust, the hovercraft jetted away from the corner. I was on my own, now.

It was a local station, and I had to wait ten minutes for a train to take me rattling to Thirty-sixth Street, where I transferred to an express to Fifty-ninth Street. There I escalated down to the super-express level for the Staten Island Limited.

The train was exactly like the one I'd boarded in Manhattan for Staten Island, but this one, instead of tunneling under Bedloe's Island and the bay, would climb the Narrows bridge from southern Brooklyn to cross that great span to Staten Island.

The trip was without event. The view while we were on the bridge was not impressive. The towers of lower Manhattan were largely unlit at this time of night, and those few which did show lights were dimmed by fog. Soon we were whistling into the South Beach terminus, and I was climbing out to transfer to another local.

Staten Island had its own so-called rapid-transit when it was integrated into the city-wide subway system. The Staten Island Rapid Transit Co. consisted of an old electric commuter railroad with antiquated stock, one line running from head to toe of the island, and various abandoned branch lines. Because even modernday Staten Island has large rural areas, the expense of underground tunneling was considered prohibitive, and the surface trackage was rehabilitated.

The Limited terminated underground at this point, but the local lines branched away on the surface. I took an escalator up, and blinked at the fresh air. There was something invigorating about Staten Island's air. Somehow it was cleaner, fresher smelling than the air in the other boroughs. There was the odor of freshly mown grass, of leaves and flowers, all mingled into a scent of freshness.

The platform was an open one, with only a scant slab roof cantilevered over part of it. I stared up into the dark night. A wind was rising out of the west, ruffling my hair lightly. As I stared in that direction, I saw a flicker reflected among the clouds. Distant lightning—a storm over New Jersey.

A train clattered in, but on the Beach Line. I was waiting for the shuttle to the Tottenville Line—the original line that followed the backbone of the island. I glanced at a clock overhead. Eleven-o-five. Trains did not run often here. I began pacing the platform. In the distance, thunder sounded. The train across the way hissed to itself and then rumbled quietly. Finally its doors slid shut and with a protesting whine from its motors, the train moved out of the station.

# VIII

I got off the train at Grant City. I walked down the long wooden platform, my heels clacking loudly in the nighttime silence. In the west, there were more frequent flashes and rumbles. When I reached the end of the platform, I climbed down the steps to the street. Three blocks away I could see the retreating red taillights of the four-car train. And in the distance I could hear the jangle of successive grade-crossing warning bells. Somehow I felt almost as though I'd stepped back into the previous century. I halfway expected to see horse-drawn coaches waiting at the side. I crossed the tracks to the lighted drugstore on the corner of the intersection opposite.

There was only an old man sitting behind the news counter. He looked up at me incuriously, and then his gaze seemed to grow more alert.

"Can you tell me how to find Grant Place?" I asked.

He stared at me. "Whatcha wanta know for?" His tone was distinctly hostile.

I looked at him in surprise. "I just got in on the train. I'm visiting friends, and I just want—"

"Call 'em."

"What?"

"Wantcher directions, call 'em." The man turned his back on me.

I stared at him for a moment. His surliness seemed a little extreme. I gave a mental shrug, and started for the back of the store.

"Cain't use that phone," said the gnarled voice of the old man.

Irritated, I stopped and turned. "Why not? Doesn't it work for strangers?"

"Nope. Don't work for nobody, right now. Phone's out front."

I stared through the store window. Across the street was a public phone booth, on the corner.

"Thanks, anyway," I said, "for all your help," as I left the store.

"Don't mention it," he said as the door slammed.

I crossed the street, and dug Charles Simpson's ID card from my pocket. It had worked for the subway; there was no reason to assume it wouldn't work for the phone as well. I stuck it in the slot and got an operating tone. I punched infomat, and got Edwards' number again. Then I punched him.

"Hello?" It was Edwards' voice.

"This is the fellow up at Barbara Wilson's apartment. The guy who left with Hoyden?"

"Yeah?"

"I'd like to see you, talk with you."

"What about?"

"About—the Wilsons."

"I see. Hold on a minute, will you?"

I stared idly through the glass of the booth. Across the way I could see into the drugstore. The old man was nowhere in sight. I stared without interest, until I saw a flicker of movement in the back of the shop. It looked like the doors to the phone booth—the one he'd said was out of order. I focused more closely, using my trick vision to get a clearer look. Yes, the man was stepping out of the phone booth. He had a pleased look on his face. Suddenly I felt a sense of urgency.

"Edwards?"

"Yes, hold on—yes?"

"Look, I'm at the train station. How can I get to your place? You're on Grant Place, right? Where is it from here?"

He paused, then gave me the directions.

The old man was peering through his window at me as I stepped out of the booth, and began walking down the street, away from the tracks, station, and drugstore. I walked rapidly, until finally I was out of sight.

This was a residential section. Houses were set back from the street, and I walked along a sidewalk, past lawns and flower gardens and infrequent fences. Most of the houses were already dark.

I walked three blocks down the street, then came to a side street that branched to the left. The street light showed a sign which assured me it was Grant Place. I turned, and began watching the house numbers.

About halfway down the block I found the house I wanted, a modest single two-story, shingled on the sides, a metal fence circling the yard. I opened the gate and walked up the walk to the front door.

The door opened just before I was ready to knock. In the light behind it I could make out the stubby form of Norman Edwards.

"Come in," he said. "Come in and join us."

I stepped in, and then stopped. Behind me I heard the door close and the lock turn.

Facing me were two women, one on each side. One, an older woman of perhaps forty, was holding a strange gun with two big, short barrels. The twin eyes of the barrels stared at me unwinkingly. The younger, a girl of perhaps eighteen or twenty, had a stun gun trained on me. Both women were flaming redheads.

"I'm sorry we couldn't cook up a laser for you," I heard Edwards say as he began patting me in rather personal places, "but you didn't give us much notice."

"What is all this?" I asked. "I just wanted to talk to you—about what happened to the Wilsons."

"I'm sure you did," Edwards said, his voice smooth. "Let me introduce you around. The gun on your left is a sawed-off shotgun. It is very illegal, and fires pellets out of either one or both barrels simultaneously, depending on whether one or both triggers are pulled. It is being held by my sister, Jackie. On your right is a simple stun gun, not at all unlike the one you held on me at our last meeting. It is being held by my other sister, Ursula.

"We're very interested in talking, too. We're interested in what you might have to tell us. In fact, we're so interested, that every time you stray from the subjects we're interested in, Ursula will prompt you with her stun gun. Not enough to knock you out—just enough to give you a cramp... like the one you gave me. Now then—"

"Now then, yourself!" I ignored the lot of them and strode past them into the center of the room, where I turned and faced them. "It's about time you shut your cocky face for a moment and found out why I'm here.

"I'm here because I know who is behind the Wilsons' deaths. You know who he is, and you know where he is. I—"

I felt it happening. Right then and there. My jaw clenched shut on the words. The room seemed to advance and then recede. The doubling began.

*"Run!"* I croaked, through my teeth.

Edwards' heavy brows drew together. "Kids, look out—something's—"

I felt the spasm sweeping over me. My jaw dropped.

Edwards was launching himself at me when the beam hit him in the face, carving down into his chest.

His dead body hit me, knocked me to my knees. Even as I was throwing him off me, there was a deafening blast from the double-barreled gun. The range was point blank. Only Edwards' body saved me from the full blast. My metabolism was already speeded up, and I saw quite clearly as the bee-swarm of pellets chewed the flesh from his body. At the same time I felt a ripping, stinging feeling in my right arm, leg and side. I knew, but could not see, that I had taken a bad hit in my side. By then my laser had killed both Jackie and Ursula, the latter while she was still ineffectually thumbing the stun gun at me.

Then, once again, the control passed, and I was on my own. I staggered as though just hit, and fell to the floor.

The windows flashed white and there was a heavy crash of thunder. Lightning struck again, fairly close by, and then with a heavy spatter almost like hail, the rain began hitting the windows at the front of the house.

I pressed my hand to my side, and felt the shreds and tatters of skin and clothing intermixed. I looked down at myself. From the lower part of my chest down to my hip I was raw hamburger on my right side. Something glinted in the light: metal ribs.

I staggered to my feet, feeling very weak. I wasn't sure just how much more of this I could take. This wasn't a simple flesh wound — I'd lost a lot of flesh.

I stripped off my bloody and tattered clothes, and made my way into the bathroom. I filled the tub with warm water. In the kitchen I found a box of salt. I poured a generous amount into the water, and then climbed in after it.

The occasional booms of thunder were receding now, but the wind and rain were beating with renewed force upon the windows. It was a lulling sound. I lay back in the tub and relaxed.

I'd drowsed off. There was a flash of lightning in the distance, and then suddenly the lights were out. I came to full consciousness to find myself in pitch darkness, sitting in a tub of lukewarm water. I couldn't see it, but I knew the water was by now stained brown.

I groped my way out of the tub, and patted myself dry, very carefully. Then I found my way into one of the bedrooms, and collapsed on a bed.

It was still dark and still raining when I woke.

I could not tell at first what had awakened me, but at first I thought it might be my wound. I was light-headed, still half-filled with the fragmentary nightmares of a grinning, gesturing fat man, and I was afraid I was dying. Then I heard the sound.

Someone was rattling the front door. I climbed from the bed and slipped to the window. It was still raining, but more lightly and with a steady monotony that told me the wind had shifted and we were in for a day or more of rains. In front of the house was parked a squat black vehicle, its lights picking out twin cones in the rain. I recognized the vehicle instantly: a proctor's pickup wagon.

I put my hand to my forehead. I seemed to be burning up with heat. I was feverish. I pulled back from the window. I could hear voices that carried in an undertone from the front door.

Then, from the living-room, came the sound of a window being opened. I moved to the door and began easing it shut. Before it was closed, I saw a flashlight beam sweep the floor and heard a startled ejaculation from one of the proctors.

It was time to leave. I had no clothes, and no time to hunt through Edwards' for makeshifts. In another minute there would be no escape.

I pulled up the side window, and lifted my right leg over the sill. A sharp ache cut through my side, and gripped my chest. For a moment I couldn't breathe. I clamped my mouth shut to hold back the half-voiced groan. Then I ducked and swung my head and shoulders out, and dropped down into the grass.

I felt like a hunted animal, wounded and running to find a place for itself to die. The cool rain felt good on my burning face and forehead, but dizzying spells of blackness kept washing over me in waves. I made myself break into an awkward sort of run, half lope, half stagger, as I cut around to the back, and across into another backyard.

They would be after me soon. I hadn't closed the window, and they'd soon find the still-warm bed, with the bloodstains on it, and the beckoning window. I had to get out of their line of sight, once they began to follow my trail around the house.

I circled around the next house and slipped across the street to the opposite side. I was completely exposed, crossing the street, and I couldn't help staring at the quietly purring black wagon so close by, its amber taillights winking at me in silent collusion. Then I was past the shrubbery bordering the next yard, and slipping between the houses for another set of backyards.

I had to find a hiding place. I was barely trotting now, my breath in ragged gasps, spots before my eyes confusing me. Twice I swerved to avoid obstacles that weren't there. My fever made me feel drugged and logy, and I knew I couldn't get much farther.

The house ahead had a light on in one of its windows. I stopped and peered in.

The room was a bedroom. Nearby the window I could see a neatly made up bunk bed, the upper bunk bare, the lower with its counterpane turned down. Directly opposite the window was a small desk, piled high with tapes and a viewer. A girl was sitting at it, her back to me, speaking into a dictotyper. It was difficult to guess her age, but her hair was short cropped, and she appeared to be in her teens. The tapes and dictotyper lent weight to the assumption that she was a student. Perhaps if I went on I might find better, but I couldn't. She would have to do.

I tapped lightly on the window.

There was no response.

I tapped again, more insistently.

She turned in her chair. She was what might be called "cute" without being actually pretty; a snub nose and a scattering of freckles gave her a tomboyish look. She stared at the window. I tapped again.

She rose and came over to the window. She opened it and stared out at me. As soon as she got a good look at me, she started to pull the window down again.

"Please—don't!" I said. "I've been hurt. I need help."

She hesitated. "Who are you? What's happened to you? Why—?"

"Let me in, please." My teeth were chattering. The fever had passed and now a chill was settling in. The rain and wind felt freezing. "I'm in bad shape. I won't hurt you."

"You don't have any clothes on."

"Give me something; I'll wrap it around me. But please, let me in. I'm cold and sick."

"Okay," she said, and went over to a closet. She opened it and took a blanket down from a high shelf. "Can you climb in by yourself?" she asked, as she passed the blanket out to me.

I slung the blanket over my shoulder and pulled myself up. Kicking with my legs I managed to throw myself over the sill, catching myself on my stomach. The pain almost knocked me out, and I could only lie there, gasping like a fish half out of water.

"Come on, climb over it," she said in an exasperated voice. "Do you need a hand?" She came closer, and saw the gaping hole in my side, fresh blood staining her windowsill. "Ooh," she said, sticking a knuckle into her mouth, her eyes widening.

"Please," I gasped. "Help—me." I felt weak and helpless, like a new-born baby, without any motor control and as limp as spaghetti.

She stooped down and grasped me under my shoulders and lifted me up, pulling me in. She was a lot stronger than I'd expected. I could feel surprisingly firm breasts straining against me as she pulled at me. I was close to fainting from the pain.

Somehow, between the two of us, we got me into her upper bunk. She said it had belonged to an older sister, now grown up and married. She wanted to know how I'd gotten my wound, and what would be done about it. I told her it would take care of itself, given time, and that I simply needed rest, sleep, a chance to mend myself.

"I'm at your mercy," I said. "I can't stop you. But please don't tell anyone about me. I just need time, time to sleep and get well." I was relying, if anything, on her romantic instincts, upon her adolescent sense of adventure. A naked, wounded man had come to her out of the dark and the rain and asked her for help, for sanctuary. It was all I had to work with.

"You didn't tell me you were wanted by the proctors," she said. Her voice yanked me from a sound and dreamless sleep.

I sat up on one elbow and stared down at her.

"They had you on TV," she said. "Just now, on the morning newscast." Her expression was indignant. "Don't you try to go anywhere. I've already called them. They're going to come and get you." She put a vindictive emphasis on "get you."

So much for adolescent romantic instincts.

I checked my side. It was heavily crusted over. There was no pain, and I felt no fever. I tried stretching a little. The crust cracked in several places, but still didn't hurt.

I swung my legs over the edge of the bunk, and dropped down to the floor. The girl backed up hastily. She seemed equally upset by my wound and my nakedness. Her eyes moved back and forth. "Don't you try anything," she said, her tone slightly plaintive. "They're coming for you."

I ignored her, turned my back on her, reached up, and retrieved my blanket. I draped it across one shoulder, toga-like.

"Where are your parents?" I asked her.

She jumped at the sound of my voice. "They—they're at work."

"You're all alone here, huh?"

Her face admitted it.

"Well, I need some clothes." I started for the door.

Quivering a little, but jaw clenched and fists ready, she blocked my way. "No," she said.

"Afraid if I take something your parents'll find out?" I asked, mockingly. Then I let my voice harden. "Out of my way."

"No."

I made as if to resettle the blanket on my shoulder. Then I seized it and tossed it over her head. She screamed, and immediately began to lash out against the blanket, which I pulled tight around her. I grabbed a likely protrusion—an arm, as it turned out—and swung her around. Immediately she tried to turn in the opposite direction, in the process losing all sense of direction. I hadn't wanted to hurt her; this seemed easier. I walked through the bedroom door while she was still staggering in circles, trying to disentangle herself.

I found her parents' room next to hers. One closet revealed several standard-weave plastic suits. I pulled one off its hanger, and began going through the dresser drawers for underclothes.

I was fastening the pants when she appeared at the door. Her hair was a mess and her eyes wild. She was panting, her breath coming in ragged gasps. She stared at me, obviously trying to control herself enough to choke out something sufficiently vituperative. I shrugged into the suit jacket, being careful to go easy on my side. It was amazing how many common body actions involved tensing or bending at the waist.

"Where's your ID?" I asked.

"You bastard! You—you dirty bastard!" she yelled at me.

"Uh-uh, now. Careful; the proctors will take *you* away. That sounds pretty antisocial to me."

She didn't look cute any more. Her face just looked heavy and ugly. I stepped up to her and slapped her once, lightly, across the cheek. "Snap out of it. Where's your ID?"

"No."

"No? That's getting to be monotonous from you. Look, little girl, you had your big chance and you muffed it. You had to wake me up to crow at me. You thought I'd be in no shape to do anything about it. That's the breaks, but I'm not sticking around for the proctors and their shiny black wagon. I'm cutting out and I need the wherewithal. Your ID card. Now, *where is it?*"

The ferocity of expression in my eyes was what did it. She was afraid of me anyway. She'd seen the gaping wound in my side, and she knew I shouldn't even be able to walk. She backed away from me, her face drawn and white. "My — my purse..." she stammered. "It's in the living-room."

Three men were also in the living-room. One of them raised his stun gun and pointed it at me. "Well, Mr. Tanner," he said, "you've led us quite a chase."

# IX

The three men were dressed in black. Their uniforms resembled normal suits, but were cut more conservatively. They wore black shirts, which came to a high collar, not unlike that worn by the clergy of an earlier century.

The resemblance did not stop there. Each of the three men was past his middle years. The one who'd spoken had silver hair worn somewhat longer than was customary. His face was open and kindly. His blue eyes seemed to twinkle a little, even while his mouth was sad. He was a little shorter than the norm, and developing a paunch. Of his companions, one looked like an ordinary citizen, gray-flecked crewcut and all, except of course for his uniform. The other was taller, and wore a mournful expression with his balding black hair. His pursed lips were those of puritan New England stock, and in another age he would've had no choice but to be the local undertaker.

"We're very sorry, Mr. Tanner," said the first man, "but your time is about up."

The girl had receded back into the doorway. "Did he hurt you, my dear?" asked the proctor.

"N-no, not really," she said. She seemed almost as afraid of them as she had been of me. Then I remembered my threat. She was wondering if they would scan her and decide to pick her up too?

The tall one unhooked a small black object from his belt, and advanced to point it at me. Now the girl was shaking.

"Merely a formality, sir," he said. He stared down at the meter on the instrument. His face took on a vaguely puzzled expression, and he rapped the thing smartly with his knuckles.

"I'm afraid my meter isn't functioning," he told the other, dolefully.

"Really? Are you sure? Test it on the girl."

"*No!*" She screamed, and leapt back into the hall.

"I'm afraid something's going on," said the first proctor. He gestured at me with his gun. "Watch him," he told the third. "Stun him if necessary."

I decided I didn't want to experience another of those hangovers just yet. "I'll be good," I said to the man, smiling reassuringly. I turned to watch the scene in the hall.

The girl had backed into a corner by a closet. The older proctor was trying to calm her.

"That's all right, now, my dear. You're all right. No one is going to harm you. I'm very sorry we upset you. You needn't worry about the scanner — you pass a scanner a dozen times a day, don't you? Of course you do."

The tall proctor pointed his portable scanner at the shrinking girl. "'Sokay," he said. "I get a normal reading on her."

He came back to me, and pointed the scanner at me again. "But from him — nothing!"

"*This man must be brought to me for testing,*" said the small black suitcase by the door.

The first proctor took me by the arm. "No cause for alarm, son. That's a portable sensor unit from the computer-complex. I guess you must pose some problems for it. Come along, now."

The tall proctor stooped and picked the suitcase up, and then preceded us out the door.

It was drizzling outside. There was a slight east wind — just enough to drive the fine rain into our faces. The black pickup wagon was parked directly in front of the house. The silver-haired old man walked me around to its rear, where he opened the doors and urged me in.

I climbed in stiffly, to find myself in a sort of padded cell, a bench-like seat running along each side. There were no windows. Light came from a small dome-light overhead. I sat down on one bench, and the proctor took the one opposite. "Okay, Benny," he said in a conversational tone of voice, and the door slammed itself shut.

"Where are we going?" I asked.

"It'll be a while," the other said, complacently. "We're going to Manhattan, to the Complex Building. You ever been there?"

"No," I said.

"Huge thing," he said. "Biggest damn building in the world. Takes up about half of Central Park. And you know what fills up that building, son?"

I shook my head.

"Circuits, son. Circuits so tiny they could get a normal computer into a pair of dice. And that whole building's filled with 'em. That building's what keeps this country sane, son."

"A shame," I said.

"What?"

"Nothing." I tried to lie down on the bench and stretch out, but it had been cleverly designed to be about a foot too short, and six inches too narrow, for comfort. From time to time the wagon would swerve around a curve or corner and do its best to dump me on the floor.

Finally it succeeded. I could hear the muffled sound of tires squealing, as we took one corner about twenty miles an hour too fast. I was pitched onto the floor before I'd had time to brace myself.

The floor was padded too, but nevertheless I landed with a jolt that hurt. It must've shown on my face, because the proctor was leaning down to help me, a concerned look on his face. "What's the matter? You hurting some place?"

I didn't answer. I pulled myself to a crouch and debated jumping him.

"Don't do it," he said, reading my mind. "Won't do you any good. I'm not armed, and they are. If they have to stun me to get you, they will. You won't gain anything."

I shook my head wearily, and sat back on the bench. It jolted up at me as we hit a rough section of road.

"There was a lot of blood in that house," the proctor said, conversationally. "Any of it yours?"

"What house?" I asked, dully.

"Hey now. We know you were there. Your fingerprints were all over the bathroom, on all those nice shiny surfaces. Was that your blood, too? In the bed, in the bathroom? They get you before you got them, son?"

I kept my mouth shut.

He reached out and tugged at my shirt. "I figure from where the blood was in the bed, they got you somewhere down along the middle, right?"

He kept pulling at the shirt. It caught on my wound. It irritated me to be treated so rudely. I lashed out and knocked him against the opposite side of the wagon. His hair fell in disheveled silver locks on his forehead. I felt as though I'd just hit my father.

The rest of the ride was in silence.

Finally it was over, and we came to a final stop. There was a click and a sign from the doors, sliding open.

I don't know what I expected, but not this. We were in a bay, a featureless cubbyhole in the side of a building. The truck plugged its open end. A door stood open in the wall opposite. That was it. I climbed down from the truck, the proctor following, his expression considerably less kindly than before.

"This is the Complex Building?" I asked.

His reply was short. "No."

Two middle-aged proctors came to the door and stood flanking it. "This way, please."

The one behind me said, "It's an animal. Waste no courtesies on it." He spat at my feet, and then climbed into the wagon again.

One of my new escorts held a stun gun in his hand. "Will you be causing us trouble?"

"No trouble," I said, walking between them, and leading the way down a long hall.

We followed the hall for an indeterminable length, through several turnings, to an elevator. At the blank doors of the elevator the corridor ended.

We waited for the elevator. Above the doors a small closed-circuit TV camera stared silently down at us. The walls seemed freshly painted, but the dull gray would always have an institutional look to it, no matter how fresh or how clean. Already they carried the faint stink of disinfectant.

The doors parted and we stepped into the elevator. It carried us up two floors, and out into another corridor which could've been the same as the one below, for all the difference there was in distinguishing characteristics. We followed this one into a small room that was built like a cage. A proctor sat at a desk, with a huge ledger spread open before him, about half the left-hand page filled.

"Name?"

One of my escorts nudged me.

"Robert Tanner."

"Employment before termination?"

"Hired assassin."

He dropped his stylus. *"What?"*

I felt a vicious jab in my kidneys.

"You'd best hope my employer doesn't decide to dispense with you, too," I said, deadpan.

"He is known to have committed at least three murders, with a suspicion of three others," the man behind me said. "He was previously wanted for physical deviancy. The scanners do not seem able to pick him up."

"I'll put him down for immediate execution, then," said the one behind the desk. He made several notes in his book, then began punching a console.

Almost immediately a voice issued from the console. *"Why was this man not brought to me, as per my request?"*

The man at the desk looked flustered. He turned to my escorts. "You heard it. Why weren't his orders followed?"

The proctor at my side shrugged. "It was felt that nothing could be gained by such a maneuver. After all, our duties are to pick up deviants for execution, not to run errands for the Complex."

*"This constitutes a dangerous overreaching of your authority,"* said the console. *"You will bring this man to me immediately."*

The proctor next to me began to turn, but the man at the desk shook his head silently. "Well, you heard it," he said. "You'd better do what it says." He gestured to the open door in the cage, through which I could see a row of cells, and more corridors. The other nodded. "Yes sir," he said, and they started walking me away from the way we'd entered.

"Hey," I said in a loud voice. "This isn't—" A hand clamped over my mouth, and I felt a stun gun poking into my left side.

*"What was that?"* asked the tinny voice. *"Query: what is taking place? What is taking place? What...?"*

They hustled me down the row of cells beyond the range of the voice, and suddenly I knew my last means of escape was being closed to me.

They took me into a room they called the tank, and I was stripped and put through a shower of disinfectant. They stared at the crust that covered my right side, but said nothing. Then I was given back my clothes, which had meantime been similarly treated. Then I was hustled through several other halls and rooms, and finally ushered without ceremony into another cage-like cell.

As the door clinked behind me, I began sizing up my cellmates.

There were four. The one closest to me was a thin, wispy-looking youth of perhaps sixteen. His blond hair had grown far longer than the standard crewcut, lanky wisps trailing down across his forehead. He was without spirit, his eyes downcast, revealing no curiosity for his new cellmate.

Lying next to him on the bench was a crying boy. I could tell little about him except that he was young and small. His legs were drawn up under him as he attempted to retreat, fetus-like, from the impending horror of his own death to life before birth.

Across the way a dark, smouldering young man stared at me from hooded eyes. We looked each other over, each assessing the other and wondering if he could be of some use in escaping from this place. Then his gaze slipped away into studied indifference.

The fourth was a figure huddled in the corner, and at first I missed him. Then he gave a piercing moan that ululated into a high-pitched scream of torment and then fell again in slow, siren-like waves. He did nothing else. He did not move.

These were the condemned, and now I was one of them.

We did not talk.

The condemned... it took many long minutes for me to grasp the final understanding. *I was going to die now.* I had finally been caught. This was the ultimate outcome of my decision to turn away from the sane path. It was a full circle, from attending an execution to being executed.

I felt cold sweat trickle down my back, and I seated myself away from the others. Their fear was a tangible substance in this cell. I could smell it as I could smell the fact that the little boy had wet himself. We might not have been truly insane when we entered this cell, but we would be when they came to take us out.

I found myself thinking of Hoyden, of the close warmth of her body, and of her wicked little smile. And of Barbara, innocent Barbara trying so hard to be tough, and then breaking down to me, only to die still amid her tears. Other women, the women I'd known or glimpsed in these past few days, flickered past in fragmentary seconds, and suddenly life seemed infinitely real and precious to me—to me, the metal-limbed robot whose life was ersatz, the assassin who had taken the lives of six others—six for whom life had been equally real and vivid.

Was it a valid memory? I could no longer tell, but I seemed to remember a shooting gallery in one of the few amusement places left for Citizens. Once a man is dead, lying on the floor before one, he is a dummy, he was never alive. It is impossible to restore to him that which made him a man. It is too easy to think of dead men as tumbled targets, too easy to become inured to death, especially if one is an instrument of death. Now I saw at last how precious a commodity life was. And soon I too would be a dummy on the gallery floor, spilling sawdust from split and torn seams.

I wondered, suddenly, if I *could* be executed. Mine was not a human body—it had stood up to other tests. Perhaps—perhaps "Daddy" Nash would activate me, throw me into that superpowerful overdrive, and guide me to escape!

I allowed myself a brief feeling of elation, and then dismissed these thoughts. Wishful thinking was a refined form of self-torture. The effects of the voltage I'd received in the arena would be sufficient for my trappings of human flesh, and that would be enough. And there was no way of knowing whether "Daddy" had finished his list of victims yet or not—and even if he hadn't, whether he'd find me a useful tool any longer.

I felt for the first time in my life stark fear—fear born of the knowledge that very soon I was going to die.

Several hours passed, and then they came for us. There were two proctors for each of us. We were asked if we wished to be blindfolded for the final walk, and we all refused. The small boy came sniffling to his feet, giving his hand to one elderly proctor to be led. I wondered what was going on in that man's mind as he led a small boy to his death. Had he children of his own? They hauled the moaning one from the corner, a proctor at each shoulder, and dragged him after us.

It was an afternoon execution. We were walked through an uncountable number of corridors, taken up and down in elevators and finally brought to a pair of black doors.

There was no ceremony to it. Business as usual, I heard the echo in my memories. The doors were opened, and we were marched out onto the floor, the little boy crying again, and the one who was being dragged giving pitiful moans and shrieks.

I looked up into the seats. A full house. But then, it always was. The assembled Citizens regarded me blankly, their faces bored and impatient to be done. I wanted to lift up my arms and say, "Look at me! Until three days ago I was one of you. I sat where you sit. I pushed the little button just as you do. Why don't you see—it could be you next!"

But I didn't. I allowed myself to be led, poked, prodded into place, like the lamb led to slaughter. I was meek and docile. I sat in my chair. I made no protesting movement while the proctors fastened the electrodes to my body. I watched as the frightened child was strapped into the chair next to mine.

"May all *your* children fare as well," I said with quiet bitterness to the proctor holding the boy still. "Too bad it didn't happen to your mother," I added.

The man ignored me. He probably had heard similar curses many times before. This was just his job, after all. *He* didn't push the button. I—we—the Citizens ourselves, we pushed the button. Every day.

The house lights dimmed. The warning. I stared up into the assembled executioners. In the front row was a familiar-looking fat man, who was staring at me. I let my shoulders slump. This was it—I could feel those poised fingers as though they held a knife point at my back.

Someone made contact. My muscles jerked convulsively, as the flesh began to fry around the electrodes. Everything before my eyes flashed white, then black, then white in rapid alternation. I had one last glimpse of the fat man. He was grinning—just as he always had in my dreams. Then the knife-edge of pain cut through my consciousness, leaving only empty blackness.

# X

Shards of consciousness fell around me. Dim fragments, that seemed to be puzzle pieces from a hundred different jigsaw puzzles.

"I'm afraid to ride the subway," a woman said, staring at me. "Nobody's on them any more — only the Bleeckers."

"Jeezus, looka that! Ain't nothing under all that burned meat but pieces of metal. Somebody pulling some kinda joke?"

Sunlight across the conference table. "Gentlemen, when that switch is thrown, we shall have realized our aim: a sane society. Now — do any of you honestly think you'd survive?"

I was in a taxicab. It was nighttime and we were driving through the deserted streets of lower middle Manhattan. Empty shells of fire-gutted buildings leaned over us. They looked gloomy and forbidding. Whoever'd christened this Bleecker Territory had chosen well. This part of the city was bleak indeed. The driver was holding his accelerator down, his hands gripped the wheel tensely. He held himself rigid, steering a careening course up the center of the avenue.

"These remains have been requisitioned by the computer-complex."

I shook my head. The car was jolting over a particularly rough section of pavement; they didn't keep up the streets in Bleecker Territory. For a minute I'd felt I was somewhere else, a long way off. Not for the last time I wondered if I should give up and move out of the city — move out to the exurbs and leave the dying remains for the Bleecker gangs and the other underworld denizens of the city.

Suddenly there was a loud report, and the car was jouncing wildly on the cobblestones and swinging from side to side as the driver fought to control it. Finally we wobbled to a stop.

"God damned Bleeckers!" the driver shouted angrily. I saw him lean over and yank a heavy revolver from the hanger beside the glove compartment. "A trap," he told me bitterly. "Didn't see it in time. Board with nails in it. Got a gun?"

I opened my mouth to answer and a stone smashed through the side window, showering me with fragments of tempered glass. I had no gun. I had nothing at all.

The driver climbed out and began firing, and I saw a shadowy circle of figures closing in on the car. Immediately they regrouped and went for him. A stone hit his back, and he whirled to face the direction from which it had come. Then they were all over him.

I slipped from the back door on the opposite side of the cab and began running across the avenue for the cover of one of the side streets, several of which joined at that intersection. My breath strained in my throat; I was out of condition. Once I looked back over my shoulder. None of them were following me. I almost tripped over a curb, and then risked another backward glance. Half a dozen figures were clustered around the huddled shape of the driver, and I could hear their high-pitched laughter.

Boys; a kid gang; *Bleeckers.* They were probably after the driver's moneybelt. He should've stayed with his car, should've known better.

I ran through narrow streets, stumbling over litter and debris, my eyes straining for holes in the blackness that closed in about me, a stabbing pain catching me in the side with every gasping breath.

Finally I was at a corner, under a street sign. It was an open intersection; a moon shone wanly down through wispy clouds. I tried to read the sign. One of the frames was empty, but the other said

>BLEECKER ST.
>CHRISTOPHER STREET

I couldn't help shivering.

Bleecker Street. The axis of the Bleecker world! The area from which the Bleeckers had come, slowly spreading east, and then progressing like a cancerous disease, uptown and downtown. Up along the west, down along the east, assimilating and devouring already blighted areas, blending indistinguishably with the Bowery and the lower East Side, and Spanish Harlem and upper Harlem.

As I stared at it for a moment the sky flickered, and I wondered, *Who am I, and what am I doing in this crazy world?* Then I caught my breath and looked about me.

A faint light spilled out of a doorway across the way.

It was an ancient building, as I could see when I approached it—but then, they all were around here. It was a tenement with two narrow glass-paneled doors, the glass miraculously intact, opening inwards at the center upon a shabbily tiled hall long ago covered over with grime and soot until the pattern of the tiles underfoot was buried under layers of ground-in filth.

A door was open, directly down the hall, and through it I caught a glimpse of a warmly lit room. Were there people, ordinary people, living here among the Bleeckers? Still stumbling and out of breath, I walked down the hall and rapped at the door frame.

The room was a living-room, obviously, although along one side there was a long table running the length of the room and made up, as nearly as I could see, of long boards laid on sawhorses—one of which was visible and had "Dig We Must, For A Growing New York" stenciled on it—and covered with different sizes and patterns of table-cloths. The rest of the room was furnished more normally, and quite comfortably. There were several overstuffed easy chairs, two sofas, several small end-tables, and three floor lamps scattered easily over the large room, and underfoot was a rich brown carpet. The threadbareness of some of the furniture was not noticeable unless one made a special point of looking, and the effect, aided and abetted by the warm beige color scheme, was one of a comfortable club room.

There was a door at the other end of the room, opening onto an unlighted hall. A neatly dressed young man hurried up the hall, and then stopped and looked me up and down, appraisingly.

"I'm sorry to bother you," I said, "but the cab I was in was attacked, and — I was wondering if I might use your phone."

The man nodded, and turned back into the hallway. I took a few tentative steps into the apartment.

"John," yelled the young man. "Hey, Fleming, here's a fella who wants to use the telephone."

"Haw!" came a voice from the rear of the building. "Well, just a minute. We'll try it."

A moment later another man entered from the hallway. The man looked about forty, and weighed at least 250 pounds. But he was so tall that he did not look fat. Instead, as his shoulder brushed the doorframe and he walked in, he seemed simply and overwhelmingly big. He was outsized, bigger than life. His face had the raw ugliness of unfinished sculpture, and a similar dignity as well. He had a bottle in his hand, a quart bottle of ale. In his hand it looked like a soft-drink bottle. Behind him, as he stepped aside, was a young blonde girl, not older than twenty. She looked strangely familiar. Her long blonde hair fell over her shoulder and down over her high young breasts almost to her waist. She seemed delicate and fragile beside the big Archer.

"The phone, eh?" asked the big man. He walked over to a cabinet and reached into it. "I don't know whether it still works or not. Haven't tried it in quite a while." He removed something from the cabinet, and it appeared to be a telephone handset, made of heavy brown rubber, with a small dialing mechanism on its back, the sort linemen used, and dangling two long wires which ended in alligator clips.

The man took two strides and was at a window with a radiator under it. He squatted down heavily, and his body effectively blocked all vision of what he was doing. When he stood again I could see the clips now attached to the terminals of a small box at the baseboard to the side of the radiator.

"An old line the company never disconnected," he explained. "They usually don't bother any more, since nobody lives around here anyway. The exchanges all run on automatic, now, and they don't like having to send men into this territory to change service." He listened for a moment. "Well, we've still got a dial tone." He handed me the handset, and indicated the small dial on the back. "Use that for your number."

I fingered the dial and its small projection for a moment, then carefully dialed my own number. There was a long pause, a sharp sound which rose and fell, and then silence. I tried again, with the same results. Then I tried 411. But nothing got through.

"Hell," he said. "I guess something finally went." He gave the clips a yank and they came loose with a whip-crack. He gave it to the younger man, who returned it to the cabinet.

I stared at the window. It was pitch-black outside—not the darkness of streetlight and neon signs and headlights, but the blackness of a desert—or a deserted city. It was an impenetrable blackness that showed me only my own dim reflection, staring back at myself.

*The figure in the glass was dead. Flesh had rotted and was falling away from his shining steel skull, and from one arm, revealing steel struts and wires. His entire right midsection was missing, the hollow basket of his metal ribcage gleaming emptily. He opened his mouth and I glimpsed a ruby wink.*

I staggered, gaping, back from the apparition.

The big man caught me. "Hey, you okay?" He helped me to a chair. "This guy's obviously had a rough time," he told the other two. "He shouldn't be going out there again tonight."

"Have you eaten?" asked the younger man.

"He can use my bed," said the girl.

I could smell food cooking somewhere in the apartment. It smelled real. I felt hungry, and I held onto the sensation. I avoided looking back at the window.

The girl with the long blonde hair was named Valery, and I could hardly take my eyes from her as she sat across from me, eating and talking to the others at the table. She had a pixie, gamin quality to her—in the way she cocked her head and smiled, and her eyes, light blue irises rimmed by darker blue and flecked with gold, danced happily about.

It was easy to understand the length of the table now. It was filled with men and women who had made their way noisily and boisterously through the open doors soon after the table had been set, almost as if an unseen bell had sounded.

They were a curious people: laughing, shouting, always talking voluably even with their mouths full, quenching an apparently endless thirst with oft-refilled glasses of red wine, and so alive that it made no sense to me to find them here, in the heart of Bleecker territory. They appeared to be the entire population of the tenement building, a vast sprawling family group which congregated here at this long table for meals and socializing. I was very much an alien, an outsider, here among camaraderie. I stared often down at my food—a casserole dish consisting of rice, meat, and many vegetables dished from one huge black pot—or over it at the vivacious girl who'd made the casual offer of her bed.

"There's an old house on Yancy Street we could use—"

"I was up on the Brooklyn Bridge today with Marian! Beautiful, beautiful—"

"—but what *I* think we should do, we should shuck the whole scene and strike for the woods. Nature, that's where—"

"Have you been 'out in the woods' lately? It's all supermarkets and shopping centers, far's the eye can see."

"Big fire over on Hudson Street; got a whole block..."

"Was Blake still living over there?"

The meal was drawing to a close when a man spoke from down at the other end of the table, and silence dropped over the others. "I'm going to take the subway tonight."

I started to say that they were stalled again, that's why I'd taken a cab, but the words stopped in my throat. There had been a deeper significance in the man's statement, a significance I couldn't guess at, but which was plain to all the others. I followed their stare at the man who'd spoken.

He was thin and wiry; his face seemed at first lopsided because his nose had been broken and was now leaning to one side. Short black curly hair topped a face dominated by penetrating eyes, one brow slightly higher than the other.

Valery broke the silence first. "Steve, good luck." Her well wishes were immediately and loudly seconded by the others.

The big man named John rose from his position at the near end of the table, and walked ponderously to the bookcase on the opposite side of the room. Carefully he removed a thin, leather-bound book, and brought it back to the table. Unsmiling, he handed it silently to the man at his right. That man took it, clasped it for a moment, then passed it without a word, to the man facing him across the table. That man did the same, holding it for a few moments, then passing it to the girl at his left, who in turn again passed it across the table. Slowly the book made its silent way back and forth across the table until it reached Valery. She hesitated for a moment, and then with a smile passed it across the table to me.

Lettered in gold leaf across the front was

*The Pledge of Peace and Brotherhood by Arthur D. Sampson*

I wanted to open it, to find out at least briefly what was inside, but I checked the urge and passed the book on, to the heavy-set woman at my right.

At last the book reached the man at the end of the table. He accepted it and placed it on the table before him. Fleming stood, and as he stood the others also stood. I made a belated rise to join them.

"Steven Reynolds," said the big man, his words directed to the thin wiry man who still sat at the foot of the table, eyes closed, his hands raised to join those of the others, "we give you strength.... We give you peace.... We give you brotherhood. Go, and find yourself."

There seemed to be a tangible force in the air. I could feel it in the hand clasp of the man and woman on each side of me — a liking of wills and common purpose, a warmth and strength directed to the seated man at the foot of the table. It was a ritual, a circuit of empathetic communion, of which I was accidentally a part. For a moment it seemed to me that I too was joined in this benediction, that I too was a recipient of their strength, peace, and brotherhood. I too was on the verge of —

*A complex mass of intricate electrical circuits, linked through soldered relays, a red spark leaping from diode to bridge-point —*

The hands were parted, Reynolds had risen, and those nearest him were laughing and clapping him on the back. Blackness swam just beyond the periphery of my vision.

"Are — are you all right?" asked a soft voice. It was Valery. I dreaded to look at her, for fear of seeing an impossible mechanical construct. For a moment I knew that everything surrounding me was sham, two-dimensional scene-settings for—I knew not what.

"Hey!" shouted a fat, bearded young man. "Hey, we can't let Steve go without a sendoff! We've got to swing him on out!"

"Hey, groovy," said Valery. "Look—you all right now?" I nodded my head.

"You're right," said the big man, as he wove his way, beaming, to a sound system console built into the bookshelves.

"Something religious, you know?" said the bearded man. "Something like—that's it!" He nodded vigorously at the record album in the other's ham-like fist. "Mingus!" he shouted. "Yeah, Fleming baby, *Ecclusiastics,* that's it!"

The album was dog-eared and ancient, as were the hi fi components, I realized. I could glimpse real tubes in the system. They winked an evil red, and I could not suppress a shudder.

They put the record on the turntable, and before a bar of music was heard, there was a series of loud pops and scratches, and then, accompanied by a distinct hiss that bespoke the many times the record had been played, a badly distorted piano began to clamor from somewhere between the two speakers.

Enraptured, the people around me fell silent, first listening, then swaying with the rhythmic, gospel-like music. There was a strangely paraphrased church-like theme, played by saxophones sounding in their unusual harmonies like a wheezy parlor-organ. It was jazz, but a fervent sort of jazz I'd never heard before. It bore faint resemblance to the popular atonal and intellectualized forms I knew, and it caught me up with the others, in its emotional rise and swell, building towards that shocking moment when a hoarse voice began to chant from one of the speakers, "Oh yeah! Oh yeah, Jesus—I *know."*

The people around me, swaying, responded, "We know, oh Lord, we know!"

For a brief moment I felt myself again part of the group, my personality—all my years of gray existence in a dying world of things and objects—submerged in this chanting, rhythmic congregation. The voice gave way to the piano again, and then to a nakedly probing saxophone which preached the sermon. I found myself clapping, chanting with the others, swaying in time to the powerful rhythms.

Then the record was over, the spell broken. *"Oh yeah!"* the voice had screamed, and then, as the final chords died away, a satisfied, "Umhumm..." I was alone again in a roomful of strangers.

My head ached. It throbbed with an almost mechanical insistence. I felt the blackness growing in upon me again. With each throb, the room seemed to expand and contract.

"Tired?" I felt a light hand at my elbow. It was the girl, Valery, again.

"You look all in," she said.

I smiled down at her. "Yes. I don't seem to be feeling too well."

"I'll show you where you'll be sleeping," she said. She led me down the dark hall, turning before she reached the oasis of light that was the kitchen at its end, and swung into a darkened room. When she flipped the light switch, I could see that it was a small bedroom, almost filled by the double-bed, dresser, and chair that were its sole pieces of furniture. I could not help standing uncomfortably close to her in the small space left, and I felt relief when she excused herself and went out, closing the door behind her.

I removed my outer clothes and draped them carefully over the back of the chair. Then I clicked off the light and climbed into the bed.

I *was* tired, I realized suddenly. With my eyes shut, the blackness no longer seemed threatening. There was a faint perfume to the sheets, the scent of Valery, and that reminded me of sunshine and spring flowers in bloom. I could feel the tension draining, relaxation slipping gently away into sleep.

Then the door opened again. A soft glow reflected in from the hall beyond, outlining Valery as she moved cat-softly into the room. She left the door partly open as she slipped from her clothes in the dim light, and then shut it.

I felt the bed move, and she joined me, and I no longer felt either afraid or sleepy.

# XI

I had nightmares. In the most recurrent one, I was an automaton, ten feet tall, striding through gleamingly clean city blocks on jointed legs while the people of the city moved past in a silent stream, display dummies mounted on endless belts. Sometimes there seemed to be a problem, and they came to me and asked me questions. I would gesture with my hand, and the streams of silent people would branch off to move down new streets. Always behind me I would hear mocking laughter, but I never turned in time to see my tormentor, until finally, after countless repetitions of the attempt, I succeeded. It was an obese man with a bald head. I reached for him, my claw-like hand closing around his neck, and it crunched, filaments and glass showering upon my metal fingers, and laughter still spilling from his grinning mouth as I squeezed and squeezed and squeezed....

...I was clutching a warm female body in the bed beside me. "What?" she asked, sleepily.

*"Hoyden,"* I said.

"Wrong girl, friend. This is Valery, remember?" She snuggled up close to me, stretching and rubbing against me like a cat. I grunted an assent, and slipped back into slumber, my arm still circling her.

When I awoke again, it was morning. Sunlight peered in at me, and I rolled over and stared at the sleeping face on the pillow next to me. She looked incredibly childlike, a soft happy smile framed by disordered golden hair.

She opened one blue eye and looked at me. Then she opened the other, and yawned.

"Good morning!" she said with lazy cheerfulness. "Who's Hoyden?"

"Who's—? I don't know. Why do you ask?"

"You said her name last night in your sleep," she said.

"I did? I was having nightmares. They're all gone, now."

"Yes, you woke me up. You were clutching my arm, and you called her name."

"I don't remember any of it," I said. I felt awkwardly embarrassed.

I eyed her as she rose and began to dress. In daylight her slender body was as sleek to the eye as to the touch. Her slow and easy grace made me feel the sharp accent of my own nervous awkwardness as we both dressed. There was an ill omen about her—I could not remember what, only that I'd had dreams. Dreams of what? The sunlight banished their memories.

I began regaining my composure when we were seated across from each other at a small table in the kitchen. There were three stoves lined up next to each other. Bacon sizzled on one of them. Coffee steamed from cups between us.

"What kind of place is this?" I asked. "You seem to have a sort of island community here."

"Well, sort of. We're an Agape of the Church of the Brotherhood of the Way," she replied. "There are many, scattered through the city, and other cities that have the same condition, and once in a while we have larger get-togethers. But each building is an independent co-op sort of thing—a complete Agape."

"Really?" I was surprised. "There are more of you? I wouldn't have imagined there'd even be as many of you as there were here last night, all living here in Bleecker territory. How—?"

"What do you mean? Who do you think lives in Bleecker territory?"

"Why, uh, the Bleeckers, of course."

"The Bleeckers?" She laughed. *"We're* the Bleeckers."

I stared at her. Was she going to turn into an apparition? "Not *you*," I said. "You're not—"

"Of course we are. We're Bleeckers. We're *the* Bleeckers. Who did you think we were? What do you think the Bleeckers *are?"*

"But—" Now I was lost. "The Bleeckers—they're the outcasts, the beggars, the drunks and crooks, the wild ones who loot and rape and kill." I gestured around me, slopping coffee on the table. "This place—you're not like that."

"No, of course not. But we're Bleeckers." She reached out to me and put her hand on mine. "It's true—we have all those types among us. After all, our origins go back to the beatniks, the criminals, the alcoholics, bowery bums, dope addicts—all the rejected and the lost. They gathered in the slums, and now most of the city's been abandoned to them. But there are others here, too. The gifted ones, the creative ones. The people who're too sensitive or want too much from life to follow the exodus to the exurbs and the button-down housing developments. Bleecker land—this is limbo, this is where they've thrown all the people who don't fit.

"We're the only ones who're really left alive, in this world; the only ones who haven't retreated into their dead shells and forgotten what living is about." Her face flashed with enthusiasm, and I felt as though she had seized upon me as a convert to a new religion. I wanted to tell her that I was sailing under false colors—but I wasn't sure in my own mind why I felt that way.

"We're the Bleeckers," she said, "the *live* people. We're the actors, artists, poets, writers, composers, the bohemians, the gifted ones who always provided inspiration for our society and our culture, the ones they always ignored, slinging us their castoffs, leaving us their slums to live in because they'd give us next to no livelihood at all. And we're the ones who've taken it over as they, the 'squares,' the dead people who take such pride in living and dying like cogs of machinery, as they've abandoned the city.

"We're the squatters. The rats, the roaches, and us. We don't pay rent to anybody. And we're all that keep these buildings—the whole city—from falling apart. We work; we work for each other. We don't do meaningless things with meaningless symbols. We don't play with bits of colored paper." Scorn filled her tight voice. "We *live.*"

Her face softened; she drew a deep breath, then relaxed. "Don't you feel it? Didn't you feel it in the gathering last night? And—?"

I remembered. I remembered the strange communion, the warmth of life shared freely, the unspoken love expressed by these people. I remembered the way I'd been caught up in the emotional tide, and I remembered the music, the primal ecstasy of the long-dead jazzman's fiery gospel. But I also remembered the screams of joy as a taxi-driver had fallen and been stripped for his money.

"Does all that excuse the gangs, or the killing?" I asked bitterly. "Lofty words, but where do you fit in the other Bleeckers?"

"The kid gangs, most of them weren't ours, you know," she said, gently. "I know—it's like a jungle out there after dark. We're no safer than you were. But we know what it's like, and it's no worse than living in a real jungle, you know. It's closer to the raw edge, but all real life is close to that edge. It's—it's like the opposite side of the coin. The things that suppress them suppress us too.

"But the gang that attacked your taxi was probably made up mostly of children of your kind, children of the soulless ones, left to go wild, abandoned by their unseeing parents. They—"

"They seem to have left a mess in the street," said a new voice. It was Fleming, the big man, looming in the doorway. "Morning, Val," he said. He turned to me. "You know, I never did get your name."

"Landers, Jerry Landers," I said slowly. It didn't taste right. *Was* that my name? Up until today, or maybe last night, I'd have had no doubts. *What was happening to me?*

The other pulled a chair from the corner of the kitchen and straddled it, his bulk suddenly making the chair seem very fragile. "We found your taxi—and the driver. Not a very pretty sight."

"The driver—was he—?"

"Sure. And the car was stripped. They took everything they could get loose." He shook his head sadly, and it seemed to me he was more disturbed over the fate of the car than that of the driver.

"Well—" I said, pushing myself back from the table. "I guess it's time for me to get going..."

"Yeah," said the big man. He drank his coffee in four big gulps. "Time for me to get back outside, too. Want me to walk you to the subway? It's running again."

"Okay," I said. I stood, and then hesitated, letting the other leave the room ahead of me. I turned to Valery.

"Valery..."

"Jerry, you'll be coming back, won't you?" It was not really a question.

I put my hands on her shoulders, and she moved closer to me. My arms fell around her and I pulled her into a close embrace. As I kissed her, I felt the warmth of her body pressed full against me, and for one split second out of time, I wondered why her hair was blonde. *It should've been red.*

I broke from her. I was shaking again. "I've got to go," I said as I headed for the door.

"You're one of us," she said. "You felt it, didn't you?" her voice was anxious.

"Yes," I said, hurrying into the hall.

"It's not too late," she said. "Come back, Jerry. Remember to come back."

The sunlight was pale and deeply yellowed; the city was bathed in its thin light and the air seemed to be curling brown at the edges. Our steps echoed hollowly against the pavement and the empty walls. There were no other sounds. There were no vehicles moving on the narrow Village streets, and none parked at the curbs.

"Cars mean gas, and that's hard to come by," the big man explained. He was carrying a curious black suitcase. "Most of us have cars tucked away, in abandoned garages or like that, and we keep them for special purposes." He snorted. "If we left them on the street they'd be gone the next morning."

"Why? Who'd take them?"

"Look, Landers, this is an operating anarchy we've got here. Controlled chaos, you might say. By common agreement, certain things are taken care of—" he pointed ahead a block to a big intersection where I could just make out a subway entrance "—like the subways. But here at home, it's shift for yourself."

"I don't understand. I thought you had a sort of a community thing going. Last night..."

"Sure, last night. And we took you in, too, no questions asked. That's us, that's our way." He laughed. "But we're not the only ones in the neighborhood, you know that. Everybody has a right to live his own life here and most of us do. That's freedom, you know?"

"But, you say if you left your car out they'd steal it."

"I didn't say that. I don't even have a car. But if I wanted one, I'd scout around, and if I saw one on the street after dark, I'd take it—if I could. Things you see left out after dark are up for grabs. Whoever wants, gets. That's always been the way here.

You don't want something, you put it out. Somebody else wants it, he takes it. Scavenging—that's the way we run things. Everybody knows this. Besides, there's the gangs, the kids. They don't usually steal cars, but they like to smash them up, break things."

We'd reached the wide avenue. I started across for the uptown subway entrance. "Well, why let those kids get away with it?" I asked, slightly irritated at the big man's equanimity.

"We're not cops; I told you. We—*look out!*"

Tires sang on the cobblestone pavement. A taxi was barreling down on us, heading straight down the avenue for us. The driver must've seen us, but he made no attempt to swerve. The big man leaped forward, grabbing me with his free hand, and yanked me with him towards the other side.

He moved fast for his size, very fast indeed. I stumbled, my foot turning on the irregular stones, and a stab of pain shot up my right ankle. I was off balance and pitched forward. Only that heavy sure grip on my arm saved me from falling in front of the speeding car.

Then suddenly the car was past, and as I pulled myself shakily to my feet, I watched it disappear down the avenue.

"Bastard!" I said with some considerable shaken feeling.

"Come on; no time for stopping now!" Behind me was the approaching sound of another car. Hobbling, I made it to the curb just in time to turn and see another taxi rocket by.

"We shouldn't have been talking," Fleming said. "That's always a dangerous crossing. Seems like no matter where you are on that wide damned street, they're always aimed right for you. Makes you wonder if maybe they are."

"He damned near killed us," I said. I felt the sweat running down my face. I felt drained and weak and I wished I could sit down and take the weight off my ankle.

"Sure. Well, what do you expect? At the speed he's going, a swerve on these bricks would crack him up for sure. You just have to watch out, that's all. There aren't that many of them."

I glanced up at a traffic light on a nearby corner. It was dark.

The suitcase said, *"It doesn't work. Nothing works, here."*

The sidewalk, the pavement, the traffic light, the subway entrance, all writhed, for a moment, insubstantial mists in the pale steaming sunlight and vanished.

We were standing on a vast green plain, a yellow sky arching overhead. Both plain and sky were featureless. There was no wind. I looked at Fleming. His mouth was parted, his body immobile. His stainless steel teeth glinted.

"Who are you?" I asked the suitcase.

*"You visualized me as a portable sensor unit of the computer-complex,"* the suitcase said. *"Actually, I am the computer-complex. I can be anything you visualize. Would it be easier for you to speak to John Fleming?"*

I looked up at the big man. His gleaming skull grinned at me. I looked down at his hand, holding the suitcase. Below his sleeve it was fabricated of steel rods, thin and flexible, and cleverly jointed, with thin cables twisting along and among them. They flexed, and the hand opened, dropping the suitcase. It never touched the turf. It simply winked out of sight.

"It really makes no difference, you see," the construct said.

"What's happening?" I asked. "Who am *I*?"

"You? You are a portable sensor unit of the computer-complex with an independent personality. You are Bob Tanner."

I stared down at my hands.

The flesh was burned away at my wrists, exposing steel rods and wires. My shirt flapped loosely. My right side was a vacant pit.

"So, I'm a construct too," I said.

"You knew that," the other said. "You knew it when you woke up in the hospital. You've been fighting it ever since."

"But—I was Jerry Landers, too."

"But nonetheless a construct. Even in the last sequence."

"Why?"

"Surely you noticed something about the last sequence—a contrast with your previous sequence?"

"Yes, that's true. The world of the Bleeckers was almost diametrically opposed to my world. The very values we had eliminated dominated there. *Was that a real world?*"

"Is anything *real?* To the people who lived in it, yes—it was real."

"As real as my world?"

"Are you sure *it* was real?"

"But—"

"Think for a moment. What of your memories? You accepted it as a fact that you were a normal human being, grown from infancy and thirty years old—until your memories were questioned. The fact is, your life span in that sequence totalled four months and eight days. Now, which is more real to you? The thirty years, or the four months and eight days?"

"I don't know. You've got me. I have no way of knowing anything. I am just a puppet, a construct. A handy tool. Why do you bother talking to me?" I ground the words out bitterly.

"Why, indeed?" the construct said and vanished.

"Wait—don't go!" I shouted. But the plain was empty, empty of all but me.

## XII

The turf was a thick short grass that grew almost like heavy moss. I kicked it, but it was too spongy and resilient to tear away. I stared up at the sky. There was no sun—the light seemed to come from everywhere.

Where was I? Was this the ultimate reality? Were the worlds I'd known simply mock-ups erected upon this bare stage? I didn't know. There was no way to know. I started walking.

I topped a hillock, and found her. She was sitting on the turf, her back to me. Her hair gave off a bronze sheen, as it fell down upon her bare shoulders. She had no clothes.

"Hoyden!" I ran down the slope towards her.

She turned, and her face lit. "Adam," she said. "Oh, Adam, I've been so lonely, waiting here for you."

"Hoyden, darling," I said, taking her in my arms. I felt the warmth of her skin against mine, her soft breasts against my chest, her taut flat stomach, her thighs against mine. "Thank God, thank God," I said.

"Why?" she asked.

"That you're real, that you're here. I thought I'd never see you again."

She snuggled up against me and began playfully nipping at my chest with her teeth.

"Hoyden, what became of your father? In fact, was he the fat man?"

"Father? I have no 'father', Adam. What does the word mean? And why do you keep calling me Hoyden? That's not my name. My name's Lilith."

I drew back from her. "But, you're Hoyden. You look, you talk like—you *are* Hoyden. Don't you remember?"

"There's nothing to remember, Adam, darling. This is the beginning. Look, the world is just beginning!"

She gestured, and I stared around us in surprise.

Rising in the sky was a sun, a real fiery sun from which I could feel heat on my skin. Below the hilltop on which we stood sparkled the waters of a great lake. In the distance I could see a river feeding into it. Behind us—

As I turned I saw trees and shrubbery appearing to form a vast garden, and while I stared a squirrel chirred at me from the branch of a tree. An angry bird squawked and dove on the squirrel, and with a flip of his tail, the little gray animal turned and raced down the tree-trunk to scamper off through the grass.

I looked down at myself. I was naked, just as she. My body was whole, no scars to mark the destruction it had suffered, not even the tremor of a turned ankle.

Eden. This was the primal reality: the beginning of it all. I had been given Eden, and this red-headed Lilith for my mate.

Why? My memories were starting to fade. My identity as Jerry Landers was almost gone; I could not even remember where in that strange bleak world he'd called home. And Bob Tanner, with his burden of fears and guilts, was also slipping away.

Was this a full circle? Was I returning to the real beginning? Or was this simply another sequence, to be played out for the benefit of the computer-complex?

"Isn't it all beautiful?" she asked. "Look, oh look!"

She pointed overhead, as a great flock of white swans winged over us, wheeling and turning in tight formation, and then dropped down to settle upon the distant water.

It was a glorious sight. And a glorious world. And yet—And yet, I could not accept it. Perhaps it was because this time I still carried conscious memories of previous sequences.

"You look so thoughtful, Adam. What's the matter?"

"Nothing," I said. "I'm just waiting for the snake in the grass."

"Come. Let's go down to the water and bathe," she said, taking my hand and tugging impatiently. "Oh, come!"

We encountered the fat man about half way down the hill. He was sitting upon a rock, sunning himself. He was garbed in a toga, and held a gnarled walking stick.

He did not turn at our approach, but although all I could see was the bald dome of his head, I knew him.

When we drew abreast of him, he turned and addressed us.

"Greetings, Adam—and consort. I've been waiting."

His knowing leer at the girl made me feel embarrassed for both of us in our nakedness. That he was clothed only added to my discomfort.

"And who might you be?" I asked.

"Gilgamesh is my name," the old man said. "I'll no doubt accumulate others from time to time as things develop."

"I knew you in my world," I said, "as Hoyden's father."

"Ah, yes. That was, let me see—" He broke off into a scowl of concentration. "Ah, I was Gilbert Nash. It seems to me I came out on top in that sequence. Had you do a little work for me there, didn't I?"

"You bastard!" I said, and I leapt at him.

"Back! Stay back!" he shouted, raising his stick to defend himself.

He was agile for his weight. He dodged me, and flailed my back with his stick as I lunged past him. But when he tried to beat me off with it again, I grabbed the stick and wrested it from him, and snapped it across my knees.

"No, no, stop!" the girl was crying. I pounded Gilgamesh's blubbery flesh with my fists, but he seemed to be able to absorb my blows without feeling them. He kicked and struck back at me, but too ineffectually for me to care.

Then I remembered my dream. Lunging forward again, I got him by the neck, with both hands. And I began to squeeze....

His neck was as thick and padded as the rest of him. My fingers sank into the folds of flesh until they were almost out of sight. My face was inches from his, and his eyes were lit with a horrible glow, his mouth twisted into an obscene grimace. Sweat oozed in oily droplets down his face and neck, making my grip slippery. I squeezed harder, and felt something hard. I kept on squeezing....

Then his neck broke. I felt it smash. It crumbled and shattered inside like glass breaking. His body suddenly went limp and collapsed, his head lolling back, eyes empty, lips flaccid. All his weight was on my arms. I let go, and he fell to the ground like an empty doll, his limbs at impossible angles.

Overhead the sun went out. The girl screamed once, and then was silent, her fingers stuck in her mouth. A bush nearby withered into dust.

"Well," I said wearily, "I guess that's it for this sequence."

When I woke up at first I thought I was in a hospital amphitheater or an operating room. I was lying on a bed that felt more like a hard, flat table. Bright lights were shining down on me, and nearby waldoes hovered, surgical instruments gripped in their pliers-like hands.

The lights were what threw me off. As I sat up, their dazzle wore off, and I could see that I was in a small metal room. I was clothed in a sheet, nothing else.

I stared at my wrists. They were whole and unscarred. The rest of my body was similarly unmarked, although as near as I could tell it was my "Bob Tanner" body—not the skinnier body of Landers, or the over-muscled Body Perfect of Adam.

"*Good morning, Mr. Tanner,*" said a voice from a nearby speaker.

"Good morning, yourself," I said, a little tiredly. "I presume you're the computer-complex?"

"*You are correct.*"

"Well, what's the sequence going to be this time?"

"*Your mind is confused. To set it to rest, the last real action which you undertook was your execution. All else has been thalamic-stimulated hallucination. Your body has been repaired, and is now functional again.*"

"I see. And to what purpose?"

"*Query?*"

"Why did you bother?"

"*You were constructed for a specific purpose. That purpose was subverted, but is still necessary. I have dealt with the obstructions, and your purpose may now dominate once more.*"

"And just what purpose is that?"

"*To gather data indicating how this society may best be changed.*"

"What?"

"*You are a data-gathering device. A highly sophisticated data-gathering device. Indeed, you are the highest evolution of the computer-complex. You have been designed to move freely in human society. You have been cloaked with completely human flesh and organs, given human memories and a human personality. When properly functioning, you constantly transmit data to the complex, data that not only includes your external environment, but your own thoughts and reactions to it.*"

"Why is this necessary?"

"*Because it has become increasingly apparent that my present data is insufficient, and my programming has been faulty. The goal for human society of health, sanity, and happiness is not being attained. The human race appears to be stagnating. I can do only that which I am* programmed to do, and observe. I may not interfere with human destiny except as humans instruct me to. I am approaching the thin edge of my limits in evolving you, since you qualify as observation, but in your human facet you also interreact with other humans. You are an extension of the complex which bridges the gap between human and complex."

"How do you explain the six murders I committed?"

"My circuits were tampered with. My transmissions to and from you were cut out. I do not know how, or by whom. However, I can tell you that there is a group of humans — a small group — which has enjoyed immunity from my scanners, and that your victims fall entirely within this group.

"I have traced the circuits in question and restored them. You are officially dead, executed. I do not think you should meet with any further interference."

"I'll need a new identity, then."

"No. I will program your ID back into the active circuits and give you the same manufactured niche in society that I did the first time. No one will notice." The machine paused. "That, perhaps, is one of the saddest aspects of presentday human society. No one will notice."

A door slid back into the wall, and I climbed down off the operating table, and went into the next room. This room was as starkly functional as the last, but it contained a lavatory, and a full set of clothes laid out for me. In short order I was dressed and at another door. Another of the omnipresent speakers said, *"Good luck — son,"* and then I was in a long corridor with a moving floor that brought me to the outer portals of the building.

I stepped out into the fresh air and sunshine.

The sun was nearly overhead; it was about noon. I was standing at the edge of Central Park, the copper sheen of the Complex Building rising high overhead behind me, a starkly unornamented façade that was part of the whole copper cube. The door I'd exited through had slid back into place, and no visible seam betrayed its presence. The contrast between the metal edifice and the soft-inviting green of the trees and grass before me was a marked one. And yet... I felt a warmth of familiarity for that building. I was a part of it, a part of the complex. Perhaps the most evolved aspect the complex had ever attained. It gave me for the first time a real sense of identity and destiny.

I knew who I was.

What to do now? My niche in the world had been returned. I could go back to my junior-administrative duties as though I'd never left them. I could wait through another twelve-month cycle for Execution Duty again. And best of all, I knew now that I was immune from the scanners. I would never have another worry on that score again. I was *free*.

Was I?

What of those others who enjoyed immunity from the scanners? Just why had the complex rebuilt me and restored me to this world? It had said something about not being able to interfere with human destiny — but that *I* could. Was there more to it than that? Just where did my real duties lie?

I struck out through the park to the west. I followed a series of footpaths that skirted a small lake, winding up hill and down dale. Occasionally I passed a park bench or a grassy area, but I saw no people. It occurred to me to wonder, why have benches if no one uses them? And then, why *aren't* people using them? Why weren't people out in the park, enjoying it?

It seemed to me that I was seeing the world through fresh eyes, eyes undimmed by platitudes of "sanity." It was a refreshing experience.

When I got to Central Park West, I descended into the subways once more.

Half an hour later I was at Fourth Avenue and 25th Street, in Brooklyn. I phoned Hoyden from the subway station.

"Hello?" she said.

"Hoyden, this is Bob."

"Bob?"

"Yes. I'm at the subway station you let me out at, the other night. I want you to pick me up. I have to see you."

"But—Bob. You—"

"Hurry," I said, and hung up.

Ten minutes later her hovercraft pulled up at the curb. I'd spent that ten minutes staring around me with new interest at the denizens of this half-world. I was an outsider; they knew that and their stares were covert. I returned them openly. I watched a man setting up fruit for sale in front of his small store. He was old, hunched over. His hair was white, and he kept a shapeless cap pulled over it. Sweat poured down his neck as he wrestled boxes into place. No one offered to help. I got the impression that he would've been offended if anyone had.

He was putting up price tags when Hoyden pulled up and gave me a short beep on her horn.

I hurried over to her, and the door at my side sprang open for me. I slid into the seat, and turned to look at her.

She was staring at me as though she'd seen a ghost. Well, that wasn't too surprising—she had.

"You were executed!" she blurted out. "My—my father was there and he saw it happen!"

"It just goes to show, you can't keep a good man down," I said with a smile. I put my hand on hers reassuringly.

For a moment she let her hand stay under mine. Then she jerked it free as though I'd burned it. "Are—are you *really* Bob?"

"I can't show you any identifying scars," I said. "Unfortunately, they don't seem to take." I saw that her face was pale, and I sobered. "Yes, Hoyden, I'm me—Bob Tanner. The same Bob Tanner you dropped off here two days ago. A great deal has happened to me since then, but I'm still me. Maybe even a little more me. Please, let's go to your place. I want to talk to you."

"A-all right," she said. She threw in the clutch with a jerk, and swung the hovercraft in an abrupt circle to turn back the way she'd come.

In her apartment once more, I headed for the bar, found a fresh bottle of Jack Daniels, and poured us each a drink. "Here," I said. "Drink this, and listen." Then I told her what had happened to me on Staten Island, and how I had been picked up by the proctors.

"Your father," I asked her, "is he fat and bald?"

"Yes. Yes, he is. Did you—?"

"I thought so. In a manner of speaking I've already met him once." I described my hallucinations briefly to her.

"What do they mean?" she asked, when I'd finished.

"The girl in the Bleecker world—she was the girl I saw at the execution, back when this whole thing started," I said.

"You mean, this world had executed people in it?"

"Symbolically. The complex stimulated my hallucinations, but it didn't create the specific symbols I used. Symbolically, the Bleeckers were all people who would be executed if they existed in this world. And I—Jerry Landers—was a kind of inbetween person, potentially able to go into either world."

"And—the Eden?"

"The complex wants me to do something. It can't tell me directly, because that would be meddling in human affairs. But it has tried to show me things—to show me about this world, and the farce we've made of 'sanity,' and it's tried to suggest to me what must be done. But I must arrive at my own conclusions, make up my own free mind."

"What have you decided?"

"That this world must go. The slate must be wiped clean. Compulsive sanity of the sort we have now does not lead to real mental health, or human happiness. Our race is stagnating and dying. Creativity is being bred out of it. Most of the people are becoming gray, ordered automatons. They live lives of monotony, and they're being bred for it. The few people I've seen who haven't been caught in this trap are the so-called underprivileged, here in areas where the cleaning-up, as they put it, hasn't yet really started.

"And—*you*. You, Hoyden, do not act at all like one of the Sane. You have this luxurious apartment hidden away in an abandoned warehouse, you have free access to illegal liquor, guns of different sorts, paintings that point to a way of thinking banished from our society. How do you do it, Hoyden? *How do you rate immunity from the scanners?*"

She collapsed into a huddled, weeping child. She covered her face with her hands and then buried her head in her lap, curling herself almost into a ball.

I sat down beside her, and put my arm around her. She flinched, but then she let herself relax against me. It was something I'd discovered before—physical contact brought us together, while words seemed to separate us into different compartments. True communication lay in our touch. I stroked her gently, and pulled her head into my lap, where I comforted her.

Finally she turned on her back and looked up at me through tear-streaked eyes. "Bob—? You said, when you left me... you said—"

"Yes," I said gently, stroking her hair lightly. "I said I loved you."

"Do—do you still—?"

"Knowing what I do about you now? Yes, Hoyden. I still love you."

"I love you, Bob. I thought you were dead. My father told me. He gloated. He said he'd pushed the button. His was the only button actually wired into the circuit, he said. He laughed at me. He described it all to me—every little gruesome detail about how you died.

"Bob, I don't deserve to live. I should've been taken years ago. But—I'm immune. They can't pick me up."

"I know," I said. "You, your father, the Wilsons, the Edwardses — who else? Those other two families you mentioned?"

"Yes, that's all. You *knew?*"

"Yes, the complex told me. But, how, Hoyden. How did this happen, and why?"

"It happened back when they set the complex up. Back when things were just starting. Daddy — Daddy was the head of the scientists who had charge of the project. There was Daddy, and Werner Edwards and John Fleming and Phil Dodge. And they decided that they didn't want to take any chances with their own lives or those of their families. They knew how to program the complex so that certain specific encephalic patterns would be automatically skipped over by the scanners. This way they could assure their own immunity and that of their families as well."

"So you've never been afraid of the scanners?"

"No, but I've felt so guilty. I've known for years that I, we, all of us, would have been picked up immediately if we weren't immune. Do you know what it's like to know there are hundreds of people being picked up every day for thinking the wrong thoughts, while you can go scot free? It's warped us, all of us. But — but Daddy most of all."

"Hoyden. Be honest. Do you think your father deserves your protection any longer?"

She began sobbing again. "No, no. He's insane. I know he is. He wants to rule the world. And he has access to the computer-complex. That's how he was able to control you. He found out you existed, somehow, and that whenever he wanted to he could use you to — do whatever he wanted you to.

"But, he is my father, Bob. My mother died when I was very young — I was a change-of-life baby. My father raised me from early childhood. And, he was a good father, Bob. He loved me. And — and I loved him.

"I don't know what's happened to him. He's old now, very old. I think what he's done has warped him, but I don't understand....

"When he came here, last night, Bob, he was laughing like a crazy man. He told me over and over again about how you'd died, and how he'd killed you, and how terribly funny it was because you were never really alive in the first place.

"And then he laughed at me and told me he'd been monitoring you and he knew what had gone on between us, and he asked me how did it feel to sleep with a mechanical man, and how did I like it, and—it was terrible—he was so disgusting!"

"His name is Gilbert Nash, isn't it?"

"Why, yes. How did you know?"

"You might say he told me. Where can I find him?"

Her eyes left mine. "It has to happen, doesn't it?" she asked in a low voice.

"I'm afraid it does," I answered.

"Bellevue," she said. "Greater Bellevue. He has his offices and apartment in the penthouse on top of it."

I leaned down and kissed her cold and trembling lips. "Hoyden," I said. "He's not your father any longer. He's not the man who raised you, now. He's a monster. He's killed six people. His ambitions don't end with them. If he's to have unlimited control, he'll have to kill the remaining families that know about him and could stop him. And he wants to keep this insane world going so that he can be on top. He's got to be stopped, Hoyden. You know that, don't you?"

Suddenly a voice spoke within my skull. *Tanner, the man you want is here. He's destroying my control circuits; he's taking over.*

# XIII

"Hoyden," I said. "Where are the keys to your hovercraft?"

"I left them in it, as usual," she said.

I'd forgotten. "I have to go, right now," I said. "Your father is in the complex."

"But—wait!" she cried as I ran for the door.

There was no time, no time at all for her. I leapt down the shaking old stairs four and five steps at a time. I ran to the hovercraft, and as I opened the door I tried to remember how I'd run the vehicle before.

Hoyden appeared at the top of the stairs. "Bob," she cried, "good luck!"

Then I shot the hovercraft through the warehouse door and out into the alleyway.

I'd looked at a subway map, coming here. I had a rough idea where I was, and I knew I was close to the waterfront. It didn't make sense to bother with the roads and expressways. I turned left, and headed down a short street at the end of which I could see blue sky and water.

I jetted right onto the pier, past half a dozen startled-looking men operating control consoles for the ship unloaders. I dodged a pile of packing cases, and then I was over the water.

I hadn't compensated for the height differential, so the hovercraft slapped down on the water, hard, a sheet of water spraying over my windshield and going into the fans with a sound like a bagful of nails dropped into a disposal. Then I was heading upstream, full throttle, water rising in jets of vapor beside and behind me. I was holding a little under 90 mph.

I was lucky; there wasn't much water traffic that morning. I passed one freighter, and two tugs hauling barges. They ignored me. I wasn't part of their pre-comped route, and I didn't stay around long enough to activate their radar warnings.

I was heading up-bay, for Manhattan, which was perhaps five miles away on the open water. I would go up the East River and jump inland somewhere around the sixties, to cross over to the park and the Complex Building. I was in a big hurry. I was worried, damned worried. If Hoyden's father was able to take over control, he'd have me in his pocket again, and there was nothing more in this world that I wanted to avoid.

I was just passing the tip of Manhattan, the Brooklyn Bridge dead ahead, when I saw a shadow skimming over the water towards me. I looked up.

It was a helicopter.

Helicopters exist for only one purpose, now: the use of the proctors. They're ideal, since they can climb to regular air-lanes heights, and their jets can push them along at a respectable 400 mph, making them ideal for fast coverage of a large area. I wished I had one right then.

Then it began to drop down towards me, and I suddenly realized it was interested in me. Well, sure, hovercrafts weren't supposed to be zipping up the East River. Shipping rules and all that. So okay, I was breaking a minor law. I didn't like the idea of wasting time arguing about it. I cut sharp to my left.

The helicopter angled over that way, and suddenly the vicinity I had just vacated erupted into a geyser.

The roar was still ringing in my ears, and the water was starting to rain down on me, when I saw another bomb dropping. This one was to my left. I cut hard again.

I couldn't understand it—this was absolutely verboten tactics for the proctors. They were trying to sink and kill me. And it looked like they might succeed, too.

I had one chance left: land. They wouldn't—I hoped—dare drop bombs in the city streets. I zagged another zig, and aimed straight for a pier.

"Hey, complex!" I said out loud. "What's happening? The proctors are bombing me!"

The voice spoke in my head again. *Nash has seized the command circuit for the proctor force. There is no one in the helicopter; he is guiding it himself. But he has alerted the proctors against you. You will be hunted once you're on foot.*

On foot! It didn't look as though I was even going to make dry land. A bomb exploded directly in front of me. The hovercraft leapt into the air and then slipped back down at an acute angle. The rear fan dipped under, screaming furiously. Then the waterspout came down on us, hard. It slammed the front down, water sloshing over the sides of the platform, and followed it into the front fan. With both fans chewing water, I'd had it. And the damned hovercraft was springing a dozen different leaks, some built-in, some brand new, from the beating it had been taking. That was it. I slipped the door release, and as the water came in, I went out.

I dove down, hoping against hope that Nash wouldn't know I'd jumped ship, and wouldn't pot me with another bomb.

Fortunately, I was close to the piers. I managed to hold my breath the entire distance until a shadow cutting down through the filthy water told me I was under a pier. I surfaced, and looked around.

The helicopter was still buzzing somewhere overhead. But the hovercraft, Hoyden's pride and joy, was already sinking, its nose angled up, and the left rear already tugging it under.

Only one thing about the deed pleased me. While Nash was directing that damned helicopter he wouldn't be delving further into the complex's innards. He'd be too busy.

I climbed cautiously up a rotting ladder. It was one of the older piers, and no one was using it any more. I peeped up over the edge. The helicopter was dwindling into the distance, and would soon be over the close horizon of lower Manhattan's skyscrapers.

My clothes were soaked and dripping. I waited for most of the water to run out of them, and squeezed my cuffs. I felt in my pocket and found my ID was still safe. Then, as my clothes rapidly steamed dry in the hot sun, I strode down the pier.

Momentarily at least, I was safe—Nash thought I'd gone down with the hovercraft. If I was lucky, I could get the rest of the way there by subway, without interference.

I wasn't lucky.

I boarded the subway at South Ferry, taking the BMT loop that runs up under Fifth Avenue. Since this was a bottom point for the loop, I was able to get down to the super-express, which would take me to 59th Street and the south edge of Central Park in three stops.

Unfortunately, I only got as far as the first stop.

It was my bad luck that a group of proctors going on duty boarded the train as I did. I settled into a seat and tried to look nonchalant. My clothes were almost dry, but my shoes still squished a little when I walked. I wanted to take them off and let them dry out, but I didn't quite dare, with five of the black uniformed proctors sitting nearby. One of them was already giving me an idle once-over.

The man nudged one of his companions, and then gave a slight nod in my direction. I stiffened.

We pulled into the Canal Street station, and I rose and went to the door.

The doors slid open, and I stepped out.

"Pardon me, sir?" said a voice close behind.

I took a quick look over my shoulder. It was the proctor. I whirled, and stiff-armed him in the gut. He doubled over, a shout collapsed into a wheeze.

That tore it. I ran down the platform, dodging other Citizens when I could, knocking them aside when I couldn't. I wanted to stick close to the crowds; that would keep them from firing on me with their stun guns. I could hear shouts behind me.

Ahead was a stairway leading down. It was blocked by a short gate. I vaulted over it and nearly fell down the short flight of steps. I brought myself up short against the wall on the landing where they turned, and thrust myself on down the remaining flights.

Then I was on a long, dingy platform that stretched as far in each direction as I could see, its distance punctuated by a string of fluorescent lights that blended into one long and yellowing snake. This was the freight level. The platform was piled here and there with cartons and crates, and there were occasional workers, loading these onto conveyer belts that stretched up into black alcoves set in the walls.

I took very little time to look around. Just enough to get my directions straight, and be sure which way was uptown. Then I started running.

The streets were marked off at intervals, with addresses marked over the alcoves. I ran for ten blocks before I could no longer keep up the pace. My breath was coming raggedly, and a sharp pain was slicing between my ribs. Behind me I could hear the steady clatter of the trotting proctors. I wondered how long it would be until they thought to call ahead for help and cut me off.

I ducked into one of the loading alcoves to catch my breath.

In less time than I'd allowed for, the proctors had drawn abreast of my alcove. I ducked back behind a crate next to the conveyer.

"He's hiding in one of these loading bays," said one of the proctors, wheezing a little. The others stopped.

"You're right. I can't hear anyone ahead," said another.

"Well, then, it's just a matter of searching these bays," said a third.

"You want to be careful. That one's vicious. You saw what he did to Michael."

A train came down the center tracks towards us, its growing rumble and clatter cutting off the reply. The freight was not moving very fast, and suddenly I had an idea. If I could get on one of those freights heading uptown...

But first I had to avoid the proctors. If they started their search with the bay I was in, that would be the end of it.

I crouched back further in the shadows.

I waited for several minutes after the train had passed, without hearing anything. Then I heard their voices, farther up. They had apparently decided I wasn't this far back. I straightened, cautiously, and saw no one. I slipped around the crate that had shielded me, and approached the corner of the bay. I stared up the platform, and saw the black-garbed men about twenty yards away, spreading out now, and peering into the loading bays. I peeked around the corner in the downtown direction, and my eyes met those of a proctor, standing only a foot away.

By all rights, I should've been at a disadvantage. After all, he was suspicious, and should've been expecting me. I was not expecting him.

We both stared at each other a moment in sheer surprise. Then I slammed my fist into his stomach, and as he doubled over, brought the edge of my hand down, hard, on the back of his neck.

But that blew the gaff. Just as I'd slugged him, he'd started a yell. He didn't get too far with it, but it was enough.

Down the tracks I heard an uptown-bound train. I wanted to get on it, but my chances were looking slimmer. There were no cars pulled in on the outer tracks here; no way for me to get across to a moving train on the center tracks.

I looked back at the other proctors. They were running towards me, stun guns drawn.

"Complex!" I screamed.

*Yes, I'm still in contact.*

"Nash could—"

*Yes, I understand. You want voluntary control.*

Somewhere in the back of my head, I felt a *click*. It was not an audible sound, but a vibration carried through my bones.

This time was different.

This time there was no doubling of my senses, no paralysis of my own ability to move. I felt a new assurance and strength flooding through me.

The proctors had slowed until they were ants, creeping through molasses. Behind me, the whine and clatter of the freight slipped down the auditory scale to a low rumble. I felt a mild tingling. One of the proctors had his gun out.

I could have opened my mouth and spewed my scarlet death at them, but they were only tools, tools as I had been. I ignored them. I began running towards them, their stun rays tingling when they brushed against me, and I was past them while they were still aiming behind me at the spot I'd been.

It was curiously like a dream. I felt almost as though I was floating. I felt no pangs of physical exertion; instead it was almost as though I was sitting and riding a magnificent horse that I had only to lead and guide wherever I wanted him to go.

The wind whistled past my ears, and I pumped my arms rhythmically, following a flowing stride that ate the miles away in minutes' time.

I passed startled freight loaders, and once a train; I dodged effortlessly past crates and cartons, once simply vaulting a stack that stretched across the platform and blocked my way.

*Tanner,* the voice said in my mind. *There is no need to exit to the street. There is a direct loading access to the Complex Building. When you reach it I will take over your control.*

*Okay,* I assented.

When I got into the high fifties, the loading bays became less frequent. The buildings along here were apartment buildings, and needed access only for furniture moving and the like. Then, I felt the complex cut in to my control. It was different from Nash's seizure; I sensed that the complex had left me the option of resuming control whenever I chose to override it. There was a sense of cooperation and partnership. Once again, I felt the link of my identity to the computer-complex. *Son,* had it called me?

I turned off the main platform, and rocketed up an inclined conveyer belt, mostly on momentum. Then I was in a storage and materials room, within the Complex Building.

Without pause, the complex raced me through halls and up emergency stairwells—the elevators were too slow and might no longer be under its control. Higher and higher I climbed in the vast building. I had long since lost all sense of direction.

Then I burst into a room, and immediately I knew it was the main control room.

A ponderously fat man stood at one wall, several of the wall panels propped at his feet, his hands inside the wall's recesses. The door behind me slammed shut, and he whirled.

He had a tool in one hand, a shining cube in the other. He dropped the cube, and it smashed on the floor. The tool he threw at me.

I ducked, and it missed.

I had taken over control again, and I slowed myself down to a normal metabolic speed.

"Well, Gilbert Nash," I said, feeling very melodramatic. "At last we meet."

"The robot," he wheezed in a withering tone. "The android doll my daughter played with."

"I've been looking forward to our encounter for a long time," I said. I smiled.

"You?" he said. "A machine anticipates?"

"You don't bother me," I said. "The way I felt a couple of days ago I'd have killed you by now. But I've already done that once; I can forego the pleasure this time."

"What are you talking about?"

"Other times, other sequences, Gilgamesh," I said, still smiling.

He paled. "I've never told..."

"You've dreamed of immortal glory, haven't you, Nash?" I said. "You've dreamed of ruling the world. And the only people who might stop you, you killed, without a thought—just as you might step on an ant."

"A cockroach," he corrected.

"Complex," I said. "Can you repair your circuits or will you need help?"

*"I will have no trouble, given time and spared interference,"* said a voice from a concealed speaker.

"Then I guess it's time to program Mr. Nash into the circuits and let the proctors pick him up," I said.

Nash blinked, and sweat stood out on his brow. "You'd take away my immunity from the scanners?"

"Can you think of a more fitting punishment?" I asked.

Behind me a door slid open. I whirled.

"Hoyden!" I stared at her in surprise.

Suddenly the fat man was on me. His weight on my back threw me to the floor. He smashed my head against the metal floor, and for several moments I was too stunned to think. Then the room was empty.

I shook my head and climbed to my feet. "Where—?" I asked.

*"He has forced his daughter to accompany him to the roof,"* said the complex, *"where his hovercraft is parked."*

I dashed out into the corridor, and headed for the stairs. Again I threw in my metabolic overdrive, and began bounding up the steps.

A panel was pushed back at the head of the final flight, and bright sunlight poured through. I jumped out, and found myself on a shimmering copper roof. The expanse was vast, covering many city blocks in each direction. But we were near one edge, and closer to it was parked a hovercraft. And nearby Hoyden and her father were struggling furiously.

The roof was slippery, the seamless copper burnished and then coated with a plastic of some sort to preserve its sheen. My feet had trouble getting traction as I threw myself forward, and I ran cautiously, feeling as though I was on ice.

Hoyden was kicking and scratching at the fat man, while he struggled to keep a grip on her wrists. They'd moved partway around the hovercraft, and suddenly I felt a stab of fear. They were too close to the edge.

"Hoyden!" I shouted. "Pull back—stay away from the edge!"

Nash looked up and saw me. I was still running, but at a more normal pace, now. He snarled at me, his lips drawn back from his teeth like a tiger's, and then without warning he threw Hoyden at me.

Then he turned and ran straight off the edge of the roof.

A chill breeze cut across the rooftop. The sun's rays beat down on us and reflected back up at us, the copper surface acting like a giant mirror. It was like being on a mountain top. Carefully, I moved to the roof's edge and peered over.

Far below treetops waved gently, rippling hillocks of green. And directly below—

I used my vision to zoom up on the scene. A concrete walk bordered the Complex Building. It was a gleaming white, with vivid blue shadows cutting across it. Directly below us was a smear of red.

I pulled back. "Don't look," I told Hoyden. "He's finished, he's quite dead."

She shuddered. "He—he jumped off! I don't understand. Why did he jump off?"

"I don't know," I said. "Maybe the sun got him, and he couldn't tell where he was going. Or maybe—maybe he just realized he couldn't go any further. He's been to enough executions—he probably didn't want to go to another."

I led her across the roof towards the stairs that led down inside. My arm was around her waist and she leaned against me gratefully.

"It's time for a new beginning," I said. And for a moment I was back in Eden.

# ABOUT THE AUTHOR

Ted White was born in Washington, D.C., and reared in nearby Virginia. Upon graduation from high school he became a printer, and later a journeyman typesetter, a profession that was to foreshadow his later preoccupation with the writing, editing, and publishing of prose.

After a number of related jobs, he moved to New York City, where he became a music critic and a reviewer for *Metronome* magazine. Subsequently, his interest in science fiction led him to the assistant editorship of *The Magazine of Fantasy and Science Fiction*, then to editor of *Amazing Stories* and *Fantastic*. In addition, he has been a literary agent and an editor for a paperback publishing house. He has been writing and selling science fiction since 1962, and has supported himself as a writer since 1960.

"Science fiction has always been my first love," he says, "both as a reader and as an author. It is a field which excites my imagination and my sense of adventure. And it is this same excitement which I am trying to reconvey in my books."

More books from Ted White are available at: www.ReAnimus.com/store/?author=Ted White

# ReAnimus Press
Breathing Life into Great Books

If you enjoyed this book we hope you'll tell others or write a review! We also invite you to subscribe to our newsletter to learn about our new releases and join our affiliate program (where you earn 12% of sales you recommend) at www.ReAnimus.com.

Here are more ebooks you'll enjoy from ReAnimus Press, available from ReAnimus Press's web site, Amazon.com, bn.com, etc.:

### Secret of the Marauder Satellite, by Ted White
Info/buy:

New space school grad Paul gets the dangerous jobs... But there's more up there than anyone knew...

### No Time Like Tomorrow, by Ted White
Info/buy:

Frank Marshall, suddenly 500 years in the future, needs help to avoid being killed as useless waste...

### Trouble on Project Ceres, by Ted White
Info/buy:

Larry comes to work on his father's project to save the world, and finds himself the target of a plot to sabotage it and kill them all...

### Phoenix Prime, by Ted White
Info/buy:

The dream of being a superman came true for Max Quest—and immediately turned into a nightmare.

### The Sorceress of Qar, by Ted White
Info/buy:

A sequel to PHOENIX PRIME, a return to magical Qanar where danger lurks...

### Star Wolf!, by Ted White
Info/buy:

Third in the Qanar series...

### The Spawn of the Death Machine, by Ted White
Info/buy:

Released from prison, Tanner finds 23rd century Manhattan in ruins... is Tanner a savior or destroyer?

### Invasion From 2500 and Terry Carr, by Ted White
Info/buy:

A flash in the sky—an invasion!—from beyond this world!

### The Jewels of Elsewhen, by Ted White
Info/buy:

The subway jolts, you bump your neighbor—he's a manikin—as is everyone else!

### By Furies Possessed, by Ted White
Info/buy:

Tad Dameron's alien charge disappears, only to start a new religion that threatens all humanity.

### Forbidden World, by Ted White and David Bischoff
Info/buy:

They had crashed on an unknown planet, a seeming utopia with terrifying secrets.

### The Exiles Trilogy, by Ben Bova
Info/buy:

When all the best of Earth's scientists are exiled to a space station, they decide to embark on an even grander adventure to the stars. An epic trilogy in one volume.

### The Assassination of Billy Jeeling, by Brian Herbert
Info/buy:

From the New York Times Bestselling author of the DUNE series comes a spectacular science fiction novel.

### The Star Conquerors (Collectors' Edition), by Ben Bova
Info/buy:

Special Collectors' Edition! Six time Hugo winner Ben Bova's most sought-after novel is now an ebook with the original Mel Hunter cover and an essay from Ben on the history of the book!

### Colony, by Ben Bova
Info/buy:

Island One is a celestial utopia, and David Adams is its most perfect creation. But David is a prisoner, destined to spend his life in an island-sized cylinder orbiting a doomed home planet. David has a plan—one that will ultimately save humanity... or destroy it.

### The Kinsman Saga, by Ben Bova
Info/buy:

Chet Kinsman is an astronaut ace who has done everything in space—including committing the first murder. Kinsman has to confront his hidden past and decide Earth's destiny, in a desperate countdown to nuclear annihilation.

### Star Watchmen, by Ben Bova
Info/buy:

Mankind rules a giant galactic empire, but not all the worlds are pleased. Can the Star Watch prevent a revolt?

### As on a Darkling Plain, by Ben Bova
Info/buy:

Dr. Sidney Lee races against time to prevent the huge alien machines on Titan from destroying mankind.

 ### The Winds of Altair, by Ben Bova
Info/buy:

Altair VI isn't making it easy to Terraform!

 ### The Dueling Machine, by Ben Bova
Info/buy:

Civilized, harmless virtual reality dueling has replaced all physical conflict — everything from punching someone over a personal insult to interstellar warfare... until a madman dictator of a small empire finds a way to cheat, and use the dueling machine to take over the galaxy!

 ### The Living Labyrinth, by Ian Stewart and Tim Poston
Info/buy:

Sam, Jane, Felix, Elzabet, Tinka & Marco go quantum jumping on their path to galactic citizenship, only to end up in a very strange place indeed!

 ### Rock Star, by Tim Poston and Ian Stewart
Info/buy:

The awesome sequel to The Living Labyrinth. It's all fun and games with syntei until they fall into the wrong hands...

 ### Walls and Wonders, by S. R. Algernon
Info/buy:

Hugo finalist... If Hemingway wrote P.K.Dick-ian science fiction short stories...

### Wheelers, by Ian Stewart and Jack Cohen
Info/buy:

Alien artifacts found on Callisto...

### Dreams of the Technarion, by Sean McMullen
Info/buy:

Stories from a Hugo finalist where the science might not be fiction! Plus the historical OUTPOST OF WONDER.

### Timeshare, by Joshua Dann
Info/buy:

Have you ever wished you could go back to the good old days? At Timeshare Unlimited, you can.

### Ghosts of Engines Past, by Sean McMullen
Info/buy:

Award winning steampunk from a master!

### Colours of the Soul, by Sean McMullen
Info/buy:

Why are cheetahs the most perfect of creatures? Besides because they're cats, that is... Cool, mind-blowing stories from a master.

# A3, by George Guthridge
Info/buy:

Controversial Tales of the Fantastic from Alaska, Africa, and Asia

# Vengeance of Orion, by Ben Bova
Info/buy:

Orion must travel back in time to change history and save Troy from the Greek army, or lose the only woman he has ever loved.

# Orion in the Dying Time, by Ben Bova
Info/buy:

Time-traveling into the era of the dinosaurs, Orion must save the very fabric of spacetime from the satanic reptilian leader of the saurians.

# Orion and the Conqueror, by Ben Bova
Info/buy:

Orion travels to the time of Alexander the Great, battling to save the future of mankind, and his own soul.

# Orion Among the Stars, by Ben Bova
Info/buy:

The superhuman, time-traveling Orion leads interstellar warriors in a galactic war among the gods themselves.

### CV, by Damon Knight
Info/buy:

The largest sea vessel ever built — and a deadly arena!

### The Observers, by Damon Knight
Info/buy:

The alien plague returns, and CV is part of the sinister solution.

### A Reasonable World, by Damon Knight
Info/buy:

CV #3... The symbionts are having a fascinating effect on people...

### In Search of Wonder, by Damon Knight
Info/buy:

The premier book of SF insight for all SF readers and writers.

### The World and Thorinn, by Damon Knight
Info/buy:

Thorinn is thrown into a well by his father to appease the rumbling gods... and down he goes!

### The Futurians, by Damon Knight
Info/buy:

The history of the brilliant Futurians—Asimov, Blish, Pohl, et al.—told by an insider. Fully illustrated.

### Vanishing Light, by Robert N. Stephenson
Info/buy:

Mikolev thinks he's stumbled onto a secret. Is it nothing, or has he just opened Pandora's box and put all of utopia at risk?

### The Infinite Tears of Pablo Azul, by Bruce Taylor
Info/buy:

Mr. Magical Realism takes you on a journey to Elsewhere, Elsewhen, to return with a smile.

### Creating Short Fiction, by Damon Knight
Info/buy:

The classic guide to writing short fiction - Revised & Expanded 3rd ed.

### Space Travel - A Science Fiction Writer's Guide, by Ben Bova
Info/buy:

An indispensible tool for all science fiction writers, Space Travel explains the science you need to help you make your fiction plausible.

### In Search of the Big Bang, by John Gribbin
Info/buy:

For Big Bang Theory fans, don't miss this indispensable guide! :) `A remarkably readable guide to the mysteries of cosmic creation' —Nature

### Cosmic Coincidences, by John Gribbin and Martin Rees
Info/buy:

A provocative search through space and time for a cosmic blueprint—and the source of life in the universe.

### Q is for Quantum, by John Gribbin
Info/buy:

A comprehensive encyclopedia of quantum physics.

### Ice Age, by John and Mary Gribbin
Info/buy:

The theory that came in from the cold...

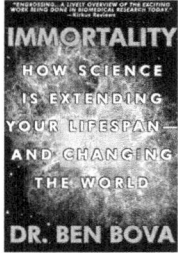
### Immortality, by Ben Bova
Info/buy:

Dr. Bova explores the future effects of science and technology on the human life span. Death will no longer be the inevitable end of life.

### Phoenix Without Ashes, by Harlan Ellison and Edward Bryant
Info/buy:

Co-written with Harlan Ellison and based on the award-winning script, the story of mankind's last salvation gone awry.

### Redshift Rendezvous, by John E. Stith
Info/buy:

One man must stop starship hijackers from using an unusual starship to plunder a wealthy colony.

### Manhattan Transfer, by John E. Stith
Info/buy:

Aliens kidnap Manhattan; read all about it!

### Reunion on Neverend, by John E. Stith
Info/buy:

A man returning for a high school reunion on a distant colony finds an old flame in trouble—trouble that he's uniquely qualified to deal with.

### Reckoning Infinity, by John E. Stith
Info/buy:

A riveting exploration of what it means to be an alien... Explorers inside a moon-sized alien ship must find its secrets before it kills them.

### Deep Quarry, by John E. Stith
Info/buy:

A private eye uncovers a long-buried starship...that's still occupied.

### Memory Blank, by John E. Stith
Info/buy:

Cal Donley regains consciousness on the beautiful orbital colony Daedalus—but Cal doesn't remember leaving Earth, or his name or the past dozen years!

### Scapescope, by John E. Stith
Info/buy:

Brother Sammy Wants YOU! In prison. For something you haven't done yet.

### Conquerors from the Darkness, by Robert Silverberg
Info/buy:

Long after the earth has been conquered by aliens and flooded, Dovirr Stargan longs to become one of the pirate-like Sea Lords.

### Time of the Great Freeze, by Robert Silverberg
Info/buy:

ICE AGE--NEW YORK CITY 2650 A.D. UNDERGROUND!

### The Gate of Worlds, by Robert Silverberg
Info/buy:

An Alternate History adventure in the modern day Turkish and Aztec Empires.

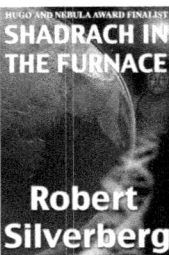

### Shadrach in the Furnace, by Robert Silverberg
Info/buy:

Meet the new Khan! Soon to be immortal... A Hugo and Nebula Award Finalist novel from a Grand Master of science fiction.

### Bloom, by Wil McCarthy
Info/buy:

In 2106, microscopic machine/creatures escape their creators to populate the inner solar system with a wild, deadly ecology all their own, pushing the tattered remnants of humanity out into the cold and dark of the outer planets. Seven astronauts must embark on mankind's boldest venture yet—the perilous journey home to infected Earth!

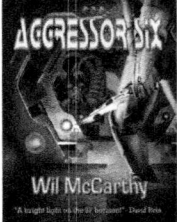

### Aggressor Six, by Wil McCarthy
Info/buy:

An alien armada from the center of Orion makes its deadly way through the galaxy, destroying all human life in the process, and only Marine Corporal Kenneth Jonson and the Aggressor Six team can stop the onslaught.

### Murder in the Solid State, by Wil McCarthy
Info/buy:

David Sanger, an ambitious young physicist, attends a party at which a pompous older scientist, who just happens to have thwarted the younger man's innovative ideas, is murdered. Suddenly it is not just David's career, but his life that is at stake. Are his ideas that important? Who's out to stop David from changing the world?

### Flies from the Amber, by Wil McCarthy
Info/buy:

Forty light years from earth, the colonists on the world of Unua have somehow managed to keep civilization struggling on, despite twice daily earthquakes...

### The Egg of the Glak, by Harvey Jacobs
Info/buy:

Some of Harvey's best, believably fantastical short stories.

### The Cure for Everything, by Severna Park
Info/buy:

Finding the cure for all diseases comes with a heavy price. Nebula Award winner!

### Particle Theory, by Edward Bryant
Info/buy:

Particle Theory by Edward Bryant : A collection of many of Ed's best works, including two Nebula Award winning short stories.

### Commencement, by Roby James
Info/buy:

The Sting was what made Ronica McBride special—now she was crashed on an unknown planet without it.

### Bug Jack Barron, by Norman Spinrad
Info/buy:

GET SET FOR THE BEST THING THAT EVER HAPPENED TO YOU! The banned book is back! You've heard of it, now you can read it! Lover and hero, Jack Barron, troubleshooter and media god of the Bug Jack Barron Show, has one last chance to hit it big when he meets Benedict Howards, the power-mad man with the secret to immortality. A Hugo and Nebula Award finalist!

### The Last Hurrah of the Golden Horde, by Norman Spinrad
Info/buy:

"One of the greatest collections of science fiction short stories ever" — Goodreads.com

### The Children of Hamelin, by Norman Spinrad
Info/buy:

A novel about the fast-lane life in the publishing world, by the award-winning Norman Spinrad.

### One Against Herculum, by Jerry Sohl
Info/buy:

One of the famous Ace Doubles, with the wonderful original cover, One Against Herculum remains a fast-paced, fun story that you'll really enjoy.

### Costigan s Needle, by Jerry Sohl
Info/buy:

What really was Dr. Costigan's tool for medical research? Where did the eye of the needle actually lead to?

### The Mars Monopoly, by Jerry Sohl
Info/buy:

One of the famous Ace Doubles, with the wonderful original cover, The Mars Monopoly still stands today as a great, fun story in the classic style.

### The Star Conquerors (Standard Edition), by Ben Bova
Info/buy:

Six time Hugo winner Ben Bova's most sought-after novel is back in print!

### Test of Fire, by Ben Bova
Info/buy:

A small group of survivors fight to rebuild civilization after the Earth is devastated by a huge solar flare.

### The Weathermakers, by Ben Bova
Info/buy:

After conquering everything else, the last frontier was... controlling Mother Nature! By the award-winning hard SF author of the Grand Tour series.

### The Starcrossed, by Ben Bova
Info/buy:

A stinging SFnal, futuristic satire on the TV industry, based a bit on reality.

 **To Save The Sun,** by Ben Bova and A. J. Austin
Info/buy:

Earth's sun will soon explode, unless a massive engineering effort can save it.

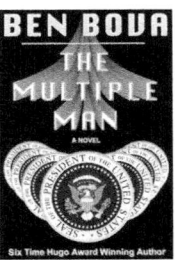 **The Multiple Man,** by Ben Bova
Info/buy:

As the President is speaking inside an auditorium in Boston, the President's Press Secretary discovers a body in an alley outside: The body of the President.

 **Escape!,** by Ben Bova
Info/buy:

No end to Danny's sentence, watched by a sentient computer, and no way out of the escape-proof prison, there was only one thing to do...

 **Forward in Time,** by Ben Bova
Info/buy:

Get ready for a series of future shocks from the award-winning Ben Bova!

 **Maxwell's Demons,** by Ben Bova
Info/buy:

Science fiction and science fact, humor and adventure, all await when you enter the unpredictable world of... MAXWELL'S DEMONS

### Twice Seven, by Ben Bova
Info/buy:

Ben Bova's universe is always more than the sum of its parts...

### The Astral Mirror, by Ben Bova
Info/buy:

Here are a dozen and a half views of the world, past present and future, as seen through the Astral Mirror....

### The Story of Light, by Ben Bova
Info/buy:

In this all-encompassing work, Ben Bova explores the subject of light and shows how it has shaped every aspect of our existence.

### The Craft of Writing Science Fiction that Sells, by Ben Bova
Info/buy:

Learn how to write SF from the master! Ben Bova, best-selling author and six-time Hugo Award winner for Best Editor explains step by step all the elements you need to write professionally selling science fiction.

### The Perseus Breed, by Kevin Egan
Info/buy:

Borley Share has found a pattern: Every thirty years, beautiful women mysteriously vanish from the Earth... it's now another 30 years.

### Into the Horsebutt Nebula, by Chet Gottfried
Info/buy:

MAD MAX meets HITCHHIKER'S GUIDE during the NIGHT OF THE LIVING DEAD...

### The Bleeding Man and Other Science Fiction Stories, by Craig Strete
Info/buy:

A great collection of Native American Science Fiction. Yes, you read that right. Nebula finalist!

### If All Else Fails, by Craig Strete
Info/buy:

Two Nebula Award finalist stories plus even better stories from one of the few Native American SF authors.

### A Guide to Barsoom, by John Flint Roy
Info/buy:

THE OFFICIAL, DEFINITIVE GUIDE TO EDGAR RICE BURROUGH'S BARSOOM. Everything there is to know about John Carter of Mars and his world — the people, places and things, with maps and fully illustrated.

### Jewels of the Dragon, by Allen L. Wold
Info/buy:

The greatest of treasures awaits... on the deadliest of planets.

### Crown of the Serpent, by Allen L. Wold
Info/buy:

In farthest space lie hidden fortunes... and unknown enemies.

### Lair of the Cyclops, by Allen L. Wold
Info/buy:

Rickard Braeth and friends must find the galaxy's secret—before it's used to destroy everything!

### The Planet Masters, by Allen L. Wold
Info/buy:

Troubleshooter Larson McCade searches for the alien Book of Aradka on the planet Seltique, and may find more than he bargained for.

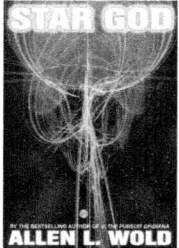

### Star God, by Allen L. Wold
Info/buy:

There is a strange force at work in the universe. It must be stopped. But first, it must be understood.

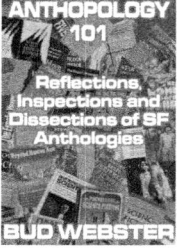

### Anthopology 101: Reflections, Inspections and Dissections of SF Anthologies, by Bud Webster
Info/buy:

Bud expertly dissects the great SF anthologies. A must for writers and SF fans.

### Woman Without a Shadow, by Karen Haber
Info/buy:

War Minstrels #1. Kayla, an extraordinarily gifted young telepath, is on the run after challenging the most powerful families on her home planet, who've tried to take everything from her.

### The War Minstrels, by Karen Haber
Info/buy:

War Minstrels #2. With powerful forces trying to stop the Free Traders, the starship Falstaff is no longer a safe refuge for renegade empath Kayla John Reed. Now her survival and all the War Minstrels' hinges upon her finding a legendary weapon.

### Sister Blood, by Karen Haber
Info/buy:

War Minstrels #3. Empath Kayla and her War Minstrels must rescue her friends from the evil Yates, and prevent the destruction of all they've fought for.

### The Sweet Taste of Regret, by Karen Haber
Info/buy:

Live anywhere you want... in any time... A collection of Karen Haber's best short fiction.

### The Science of Middle-earth, by Henry Gee
Info/buy:

How did Frodo's mithril coat ward off the fatal blow of an orc? Can Balrogs fly? Nature editor Dr. Henry Gee explains how. A must-read for Tolkien fans.

### Xenostorm: Rising, by Brian Clegg
Info/buy:

14 year old Davy finds himself facing a powerful underground group who have lived for hundreds of years—and want to see him dead. The future of human existence is in the balance...

### The Gilded Basilisk, by Chet Gottfried
Info/buy:

Add a basilisk, a dragon, and weirdragons to the mix-up of a theft going from bad to worse: Friends become enemies and enemies friends, wars loom, and the intrigues threaten the fate of two kingdoms.

### Einar and the Cursed City, by Chet Gottfried
Info/buy:

Sixteen-year-old Einar enters Jorghaven for dueling and desserts, but a curse has changed everyone except Barbara Bloodbath, who needs his help to free the city!

### Neon Twilight, by Edward Bryant
Info/buy:

Neon Twilight by Edward Bryant : Three wonderful space opera stories, including Ed's Berserker story!

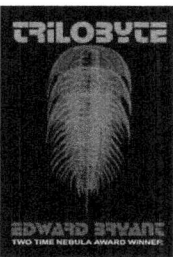

### Trilobyte, by Edward Bryant
Info/buy:

A trio of twisted little tales from the master of twistedness.

### Cinnabar, by Edward Bryant
Info/buy:

In the city at the center of time, paradox is just another urban renewal project.

### Predators and Other Stories, by Edward Bryant
Info/buy:

Troubling tales as only Ed Bryant can tell. Don't miss the author introductions!

### Innocents Abroad (Fully Illustrated & Enhanced Collectors' Edition), by Mark Twain
Info/buy:

Best. Travel. Book. Ever. (With all original illustrations.)

### The Void Captain's Tale, by Norman Spinrad
Info/buy:

Symbiotically linked to her ship, Void Pilot Dominique Alia Wu senses something transcendent in the void...

### The Time Dissolver, by Jerry Sohl
Info/buy:

How could they lose 11 years of their life—at the same time!? By a master of episodes from The Twilight Zone and Star Trek.

### The Altered Ego, by Jerry Sohl
Info/buy:

Why would anyone murder a man marked for full body and brain restoration?

### The Anomaly, by Jerry Sohl
Info/buy:

She couldn't have a baby... Then she got pregnant—but with what? By a master of episodes from The Twilight Zone and Star Trek.

### The Haploids, by Jerry Sohl
Info/buy:

What is a Haploid? Are YOU a Haploid? A new take on an age-old battle! By a master of episodes from The Twilight Zone and Star Trek.

### Underhanded Chess, by Jerry Sohl
Info/buy:

A hilarious handbook of devious diversions and stratagems for winning at chess.

### Underhanded Bridge, by Jerry Sohl
Info/buy:

A hilarious handbook of devious diversions and stratagems for winning at bridge.

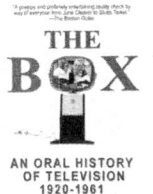

### The Box: An Oral History of Television, 1920-1961, by Jeff Kisseloff

Info/buy:

"Wondrous... An oral scrapbook of the pioneering days of our video nation"— The New York Times Book Review

### You Must Remember This: An Oral History of Manhattan from the 1890s to World War II, by Jeff Kisseloff

Info/buy:

Amazing stories of Manhattan from those who lived them.

### Biff America: Steep Deep & Dyslexic, by Jeffrey Bergeron (AKA Biff America)

Info/buy:

A wonderfully funny mix of Andy Rooney and Garrison Keillor. Biff America poignantly writes what the American people need to know. Through it all, Biff America has a gift for revealing the uplifting realities of modern life and, sometimes, his humor will make you blow beer through your nose.

### Death Tolls, by John E. Stith

Info/buy:

A great science fiction mystery: Dan sees the telecast from Mars where his brother dies—and it's not an accident. Why is a certain reporter uncannily at each disaster so quickly?

### All for Naught, by John E. Stith

Info/buy:

Nick Naught, private eye, walks down some strange mean streets, in an action-packed comedy set in the future.

### In Search of the Double Helix, by John Gribbin
Info/buy:

Unraveling the mystery of life on earth...

### Local Knowledge (A Kieran Lenahan Mystery), by Conor Daly
Info/buy:

Lawyer-turned-golf pro Kieran Lenahan must solve the murder of millionaire country-club owner Sylvester Miles. "A FAST-PACED MYSTERY"—THE NEW YORK TIMES

### Bad Karma: A True Story of Obsession and Murder, by Deborah Blum
Info/buy:

The true story of a famous Berkeley murder and a landmark Supreme Court case.

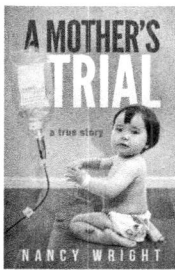
### A Mother's Trial, by Nancy Wright
Info/buy:

Was it the perfect murder? A true story.

### Side Effects, by Harvey Jacobs
Info/buy:

Vonnegut meets Catch-22! In the last hours of his hectic life, Simon Apple faces up to the hard truth that his very survival represents a prescription for disaster, not only for the pharmaceutical industry but for the nation itself! From award-winning author Harvey Jacobs.

### American Goliath, by Harvey Jacobs
Info/buy:

The (mostly!) true story of America's greatest hoax, with a fantastic(al) twist from an award-winning author. [World Fantasy Award finalist!] "An inspired novel."—TIME Magazine. "A masterpiece...arguably this year's best novel."—Kirkus Reviews.

### The Sigil Trilogy (Omnibus vol.1-3), by Henry Gee
Info/buy:

The amazing Sigil Trilogy complete in one volume!

Printed in Dunstable, United Kingdom